SATURNALIA

T.W.M. ASHFORD

ash
ford

DARK STAR PANORAMA

~

The *Dark Star Panorama* is the shared universe of sci-fi stories in which *Saturnalia* takes place. Other series include *Final Dawn* and *War for New Terra*.

To hear about new releases and receive exclusive free content, sign up for T.W.M. Ashford's mailing list at the website below.

www.twmashford.com

BOOKS IN THE "DARK STAR PANORAMA" UNIVERSE

Final Dawn Series

- The Final Dawn
- Thief of Stars
- A Dark Horizon
- The New World
- The Tin Soldiers
- Ghost of the Father
- The Stellar Abyss
- The Edge of Night
- The Fatal Dark

War for New Terra Series

- Sigma
- Iron Nest
- Royal Blood

Standalone Novels

- Saturnalia

SATURNALIA

H olly Bloom sat bolt upright in her swivel chair as
soon as the email landed in her inbox.

It wasn't addressed to her. It wasn't technically addressed to anyone, in fact, only the anonymous
audience labelled *Upper Management*. Holly had got Talbot
down in IT to set up an alert on her computer so that any
communication concerning the Saturnalia space station got
flagged for her attention – including any confidential correspondence regular employees weren't supposed to see. She
wasn't *technically* breaking any company rules, but she
highly doubted Flynn Industries would share her
entrepreneurial outlook on the matter.

Normally she deleted the emails almost as quickly as
they appeared. But not this one. This one tightened her
chest and made her skin itch. It was only six words long.

SATURNALIA COMMS OFFLINE. SEND SECURITY TEAM.

This was the opportunity she'd been waiting for.

Pausing only long enough to take a deep breath, she
swiped the email from her company computer onto her
personal data pad. Another company no-no. Everybody did

it, though. It was the only way to stay on top of your tasks without permanently setting up camp inside the office. That this was the first time Holly had done it spoke wonders of her usual work ethic.

She rose from her cramped cubicle, ignoring the arrival of another urgent message that actually *was* marked for her attention. Brian Edwards glanced up from his desk opposite hers, then went back to lethargically prodding his touch screen with a pair of greasy, snack-stained fingers. Holly shuddered. Why humanity hadn't developed affordable holo-screen technology yet was a mystery the world's germaphobes continued to ponder.

Oh well. One way or another, she'd be out of this place soon enough.

Her supervisor's door lurked at the far end of the office. It was closed to the rest of the floor, as always. She wouldn't be surprised if it was locked. Neither did she blame her supervisor for keeping it shut. Who in their right mind would want an eight by eight grid of grey, laminate, chesthigh cubicles filled with spotty, burnt-out corporate grunts for a view? There weren't even any motivational posters pinned to the walls. The paper was too expensive.

She marched down the meagre aisle separating one cluster of booths from the other, clutching her data pad to her chest as if afraid one of her co-workers might catch a glimpse of its screen and steal her idea. Brian's certainly wasn't the last stare she received along the way. The bathrooms were in the opposite direction and anyone not at their desk was not contributing to the bottom line. Everyone was replaceable, as the company endlessly reminded them. If they didn't want the job, someone else would gladly take it.

Holly paused outside the door. Last chance to bury this mad plan before she got into any real trouble. She could return to her desk, crack on with her work and nobody would be any the wiser.

No. She couldn't let the last three years be for nothing.

She gave the door two quick raps with the back of her knuckles and then inched it open.

"Excuse me, Ms. Nicholson? Can I have a word?"

Her supervisor craned her already elongated neck to see through the gap, sighed like a deflating air mattress and waved her inside. Her windowless office was lined with fake oak panels and smelled strongly of artificial pine cone.

"Yes, Bloom, fine. Is this about the Leviathan report? It's due today, you know."

"I'll have it finished by the end of business." Holly found herself standing almost to attention in front of Ms. Nicholson's desk. "No, this is about the, erm... the Saturnalia. You're sending a team to fix their communications issue, right?"

"How do you know about that?" Frowning, Aria Nicholson gave her own workstation a quick check. "That order's barely been in my inbox three minutes. Are you sticking your nose places it doesn't belong, Bloom?"

Holly swallowed hard and tried to keep her hands from fidgeting.

"I was rather hoping I could volunteer for the assignment, Ms. Nicholson."

"Volunteer? Why on earth would you want to do that?"

"You *are* sending an analyst, aren't you?"

"Of course we are. How else is the company supposed to know how much this is going to cost us? I'm just questioning why you, of all people, should want the assignment. You're not exactly the zealous type, let's be honest."

Aria Nicholson leaned across her desk and fixed Holly with an expectant glare capable of wilting the hardiest thistle. It was like staring into a heat lamp. Holly cast her eyes down to her shoes before she could stop herself and prayed she didn't start sweating.

"There aren't many opportunities to travel off-world for a woman in my position," she replied, lifting her eyes slightly. "And, well... I was rather hoping it might elevate my position within the company. I've always fancied moving into the Defence division one day."

Ms. Nicholson continued staring at Holly and tapped a manicured fingernail against the faux-leather mat covering her side of the desk.

"Hmm. It's not a comfortable journey, you know. And you won't get treated like a resident while you're there."

"I understand that."

"I *was* going to send Glasspool. The boy's been before. Knows his way around the station, gets on well with the administrator. Smart lad."

Presently there came a knock at the office door. A spectacled man with fluffy pumpkin-coloured hair poked his head through the frame.

"You asked to see me, Ms. Nicholson?"

Their supervisor studied the young man without word, turned her attention back to Holly while chewing her bottom lip, and then waved Glasspool away.

"False alarm, Glasspool. Back to your desk."

"Right you are, miss."

The man eagerly retracted his head from the doorway. Holly's stomach tied itself into a double fisherman's knot. Was she actually being given the assignment? Not knowing whether to feel thrilled or frightened, she settled for mild nausea instead.

Aria Nicholson broke into a wry smile.

"I always knew you had the spark," she said, waggling a finger at Holly with one hand and swiping through the messages on her monitor with the other. "One day, I told myself, that girl's gonna realise her true potential at Flynn. Would sure be good to see another woman leading a team. How much do you know about Saturnalia?"

"The space station?" Holly pouted as she feigned ignorance. "Only what everyone else knows – it's a haven for the hyper-rich that shares an orbit around Saturn with its moon, Titan. Founded by a conglomerate formed of the richest families on Earth. Wasn't Flynn Industries the majority shareholder?"

"Second largest," Nicholson corrected her, "but Albert Flynn, God rest his soul, was given charge of the shared assets, yes. These days most of the company's focus is on constructing New Terran settlements, of course, but it also has contracts for the UEC military *and* we coordinate regular supply shipments to Saturnalia. You remember how much hassle the Bradley delivery caused us."

"That was only last week. Is this comms blackout something we should be concerned about?"

"Not in the slightest." Nicholson shut her eyes and shook her head. "Happens all the time. Something about the rotation of Saturn distorts the signal. Don't ask me why – the company's looking into it. Normally it sorts itself out after a few hours, but it's been a full day since anyone heard from the crew. Could be a glitch, could be a comm array malfunction. That's why we send a team in to check everyone's safe and ensure those rich bigwigs don't think we've forgotten about them. And while that's going on, *you* compile a report on what really needs fixing and what it'll cost the company. Still think you can handle it?"

"Seems no harder than my regular work," Holly said, risking a shrug.

"Speaking of which," Nicholson said, squinting at her

monitor, "hand all of your ongoing projects to Edwards. You shouldn't be gone more than three days. Four, tops. He can reassign them to you once you're back."

"All of them? When do I leave?"

"Six am tomorrow morning. Hammerton Spaceport. Can't leave those VIPs waiting, Bloom. Now go on, get back to your desk. I can't for the life of me figure out why you'd want to put yourself through the trip, but you won't see me pulling the ladder away from a corporate climber."

Holly smiled politely and turned to leave. She was already halfway through the door when Nicholson cleared her throat rather deliberately.

"Oh, and Bloom?"

"Yes?"

"Leviathan report. My inbox by five or I'm sending Glasspool."

Holly shut the door behind her, listened for the satisfying *thunk* sound of its latch. She paused, pursed her lips and let out a long, quavering sigh of relief.

It was done. She could hardly believe it.

Three years, and she was finally headed to Saturnalia.

She hurried back to her desk. Though she lowered her gaze to avoid making eye contact with her colleagues, she could feel their beady-eyed scrutiny on the back of her neck as they asked themselves what she could possibly have been doing in Nicholson's office for so long that wasn't getting fired. Or, alternatively, what it was she'd been fired *for*.

The funny thing was, if any of them found out she'd been given the Saturnalia assignment they'd more likely feel sympathy towards her than suspicion. For all the mystique surrounding the luxurious and isolated space station, nobody wanted to go there. And not just because it was a joyless reminder of a world no mere mortal could ever hope to experience – the last time someone returned from an off-world contract, he spent almost as long in the district infirmary recovering from his travel sickness as he had on the trip itself.

Holly burrowed into her cubicle, collapsed into her chair and stared numbly at the blank screen in front of her. Her mind seemed equally devoid of content.

"So I'm pulling double-duty while you're off travelling? Cheers, love."

Brian Edwards gave her a deadpan glare from the cubicle across the aisle. Holly flashed him a sympathetic smile in return.

"Sorry, Edwards. Nicholson's orders."

"Hey." He rolled his eyes and resumed systematically jabbing his monitor. "Rather you than me. I can't even take the shuttle to work without getting car sick..."

Holly ran her hands along the length of her cramped, plastic desk and soaked in the three-and-a-half walls of her drab, fluorescent-lit cage. Regardless of how things went on Saturnalia, this might be the last time she saw it. Pity. She'd almost grown accustomed to the captivity.

She rearranged her desk as subtly as possible. She had little in the way of employee rights, after all – no chance to clear out her desk and perform the walk of shame with a cardboard box full of keepsakes cradled in her arms, either. The violet she'd planted in a disposable cup went to one side where she wouldn't forget it.

From its spot tucked into the cubicle wall to her left she retrieved a photograph – an old-fashioned physical picture on glossy paper that had cost her almost a week's wages. A waste of money, probably, but looking at it was all that had kept her sane those past few years. A much younger version of herself – she couldn't have been more than four – sat and grinned next to her parents on the living room floor while her baby sister made a desperate bid for freedom on her hands and knees. Mum and Dad were gone now, had been for a while, but it still made her smile. She stood it upright against the makeshift plant pot.

And a flaking Flynn Industries-branded stress ball. It wasn't technically hers, but it was sure as hell coming with her anyway. It was pretty much the only company benefit she got.

Holly was keenly aware that while specific computer activity wasn't monitored – if it was, she never would have received the message about Saturnalia to begin with – but the company *definitely* had ways of ensuring its employees weren't slacking off. She'd been back at her desk for five whole minutes and not so much as disengaged her screensaver. The black eye of the security camera installed above the corner of the corridor couldn't have made the target of its obsession more obvious if it had winked at her.

Casting all thought of tomorrow from her mind as best she could, Holly took a deep breath, flexed her fingers and got typing.

The Leviathan report wasn't going to write itself.

CHAPTER
TWO

No matter what she did, the vomit just kept coming.

"Is this normal?" Holly asked between retches. "I don't know what I'm even throwing up anymore. It's not as if I had any appetite for breakfast this morning."

"Happens to everyone the first time," Carlson said as he pried the bucket away from her. "Well. Almost everyone."

"Here." Through a blurry film of tears, Holly saw some sort of pill being proffered in her direction. "Take this."

"My brain feels like it's splitting in half."

"Yeah, that's cranial fluid shift. The capsule will help with that."

Holly navigated the pill into her mouth and washed it down with a gulp of water sucked from a straw-punctured pouch. It hurt to swallow – she must have burned her throat up something rotten.

"Good. Now eat this." The same woman handed her a protein bar. "It'll boost your sodium levels."

"And that's a good thing, is it?"

"Yes. Trust me. Our pay gets docked if we kill the company analyst."

Holly forced herself to take a bite from the protein bar. The silver-foil wrapper was considerably more attractive than the supposed "foodstuff" inside. It was like chewing nougat. Or a tyre. The only consolation was that the snack was so salty she was spared the ordeal of finding out what the strange artificial material was actually supposed to taste like.

Sure enough, by the time she crushed the empty wrapper inside her fist her migraine had devolved to a mere searing headache. And it felt good to have something solid inside her stomach, too. She only hoped the rest of her in-flight meals boasted slightly better flavour.

Holly was pretty sure they'd taken off less than an hour ago – she hadn't exactly been in a fit state to count the minutes since – and already she was starting to regret volunteering for the trip. She'd arrived at Hammerton Spaceport an hour before the shuttle was scheduled to depart, which was half an hour more than she needed. Commercial interstellar space-travel wasn't a thriving industry yet, and the security desk had registered, scanned and cleared her for the flight within fifteen minutes.

The sun had been but a soft yellow sliver on the horizon. The first cry of birdsong peppered the sweet, dewy air. With no private lounge available – only someone with a few ice cubes short of a Moscow Mule would order a beer immediately before take-off – Holly anxiously made her away to the designated launch pad on foot. Though, like most citizens of New Terra, she'd never visited the spaceport before, finding the correct shuttle wasn't hard. There were only three. Far more ships frequented the facilities on the northern side of the port – military transporters and gunships, for the most part. But even then, the larger UEC battlecruisers had to be built and docked in orbit.

It had taken all of humanity's ingenuity and resources to cross the stars and colonise their new home. Having gone to all the trouble of getting there, most people were quite happy staying put. Not the population of Saturnalia, though. They'd headed back to the Sol system the moment construction of their space station had been completed.

Holly refused to refer to the vehicle as a rocket. Call her odd, but rockets made her think of explosions. She found the *shuttle* towards the western perimeter on a wide, circular podium elevated to a dozen metres above ground level. It was no small city-hopper, by any means. Four enormous thrusters bulged out from the underside of a fifty-foot chrome bullet balanced on three gawky, steel spider legs.

The bottom half of the shuttle was dedicated to just its fuel tanks and drive core. What remained of the ship was split into two sections. First was the passenger fuselage, which sported eight harnessed seats around its circumference, a cubby hole for a toilet and numerous latched cupboards for storing cargo. A set of metal rungs led up to the two-seat cockpit inside the nose.

The shuttle had been designed so that as long as it was accelerating, everyone on board would be pushed down towards the engines beneath their feet, effectively experiencing gravity. Of course, the engineers never promised that gravity would be a *comfortable* experience.

Spaceport attendees had still been hurrying around the shuttle when Holly arrived, disconnecting the fuel lines, setting up the boarding steps and loading all the necessary provisions into its hold. She trusted the pilots had gone through all the preliminary safety checks already, because she didn't know if her heart could take six hours of squirming about waiting for launch.

Four marines in black uniform unloaded crates from a motorised cart. She guessed the security team had beaten her there, too.

"You the analyst?" the gruffest and most bearded of their number asked upon her approach.

"The one and only," Holly replied, nervously clutching the bag containing her data pad and other essentials.

"Punctual. Good. I'm Carlson. This here's Wade, Lynch and Banks."

They each nodded as their name was called out. Wade was skinny and spectacled with cropped hair and tribal tattoos that wrapped across his temples. Lynch was the only woman in the group, yet the blonde towered over Wade. There was something about the butch, unkempt Banks that spoke of quiet intelligence to Holly – the squad's technical engineer, without a doubt. She estimated they were all in their late thirties, given their profession, despite appearances suggesting they were half a decade older or more.

"I don't mean to be an arsehole," Lynch said as she grabbed another crate, "but do you mind giving us a bit of space? We've got some special orders to fulfil."

"Special orders?" Holly asked.

"Not every resident has requests they want to see listed on the company invoice, if you catch our drift," Carlson replied sternly. "We're on a deadline. Go enjoy the fresh air while you still can."

And so she'd left them to it, her insides burning as launch beckoned, trembling alone beneath the silver bullet set to shoot her across the cosmos.

God, what she would do to only feel as nauseous now as she did back then.

Her stomach lurched. She doubled-over just as Carlson came rushing back with the empty bucket, but thankfully nothing came up.

"Urgh. To think I've got to survive another fifteen hours of this. Why the hell does this journey take so long, anyway? I thought the Sol system was only a few stars over."

"We're lucky to have any kind of skip drive tech at all," Lynch said. "You know the motto. *Human made, humans saved.* How's the UEC ever supposed to stand on its own two feet if we don't figure out how this faster-than-light shit works for ourselves, right?"

"Just be grateful you ain't stuck in stasis," Carlson grumbled, "or getting punched through a wormhole."

"It gets easier the more you do it," Wade said, manically scratching the side of his neck. "Look at us. We've done loads of jumps, and we're all doing just fine."

The rocket shuddered as it barrelled through subspace. Holly clenched her eyelids shut almost as tightly as she did her teeth.

"And it doesn't bother any of you that we're literally sitting on enough explosives to level a city block?"

Banks gifted her a melancholy smile from his seat on the opposite side of the cabin.

"We've survived worse."

Ah, yes. The war. It had ended eight years ago when colonisation of New Terra began, but even now many of the survivors didn't like talking about it.

For obvious reasons, everyone's rifles had been safely stowed inside a locker prior to launch. The locker door rattled irritably as if the guns were trying to break out.

"Are guns a sensible thing to bring onto a space station?" she asked.

Carlson laughed.

"The Saturnalia's hull is built to withstand asteroid collisions," he replied. "She can handle the odd stray bullet. That said, we're only packing rubber rounds. They'll leave you eating through a straw, but they won't kill ya. Can't go losing any shareholders to friendly fire."

"They don't dock your wages for killing a VIP," Wade joked. "They dock your life."

"Good one, Wade," Lynch said, rolling her eyes. "Honestly, you'd think Flynn Industries could afford a better standard of security."

"You're paid by the company?" Holly frowned. "I assumed you were sent by the UEC."

"Ex-marines." Lynch smirked. "We aged out of our mandatory terms, so it was a choice between enlisting with the local police force or going private. The latter pays better. Plus, the only way you get to see the stars if you turn cop is from your bedroom window."

Aged out. Holly was wrong – they *were* in their early forties. With new recruits signing up for an easy pay packet, the UEC could finally afford to release its troops from their contracts once they reached the big four-oh. Most pounced on the opportunity for a quiet life.

"So you served before all this, then? Back on Earth, I mean."

"Sure did," Wade replied, flashing a yellow smile. "Saw the riots, the terrorism – everything. Dark times, lady."

"Fireteam Echo, Fourth Company." Carlson nodded proudly. "Signed up in the autumn of '57, left in the summer of 6AE. So what's it been with Flynn, three years now?"

"In a month's time, yeah." Banks eyed Holly curiously. "But you're no baby, Miss Bloom. You were alive Before Exodus, too."

Holly chuckled, even as the shuttle shook.

"Yeah, but I was what, twenty when the Arks left Earth? Twenty-one, maybe? My parents won tickets in the lottery, and I was in school, so it's not like I actually experienced any of the... well, you know. All the bad stuff we left behind."

"Lottery winner, eh?" Wade laughed and shook his head. "Some people have all the luck..."

"And you thought you'd use your second chance at life to, what?" Lynch raised an amused eyebrow. "Become an analyst?"

"Hey, don't knock it. Apparently it wasn't a profession prioritised during the evacuation, so they offered incentives to graduates willing to study it. It sure beats guarding building sites and latrines for a living."

"All right, all right." Carlson rose from his seat and began handing out more capsules before his squad mate could respond. "Sharing time's over. Get this down you," he said when he reached Holly.

"What is it?" she asked, studying the pink pill. "Something to keep my brain from haemorrhaging?"

"No, love. It's melatonin. Twenty milligrams of it. With any luck it'll knock you out for most of the trip."

"You'll wanna sleep," said Lynch. "It sure beats waiting for the inflight movie to start."

"And here I was planning to read my book," Holly replied, eagerly swallowing the capsule dry.

"Sweet dreams, everyone," Carlson said, pulling his harness down over his shoulders. "Once everyone's awake again, Banks is making breakfast."

"What's on the menu this time?" Wade asked, practically salivating.

"My specialty," Banks said, smiling with his eyes closed. "Sausage and egg a la protein pouch."

"Can it, lads." Carlson flicked a switch on a wall-mounted control panel beside him and all but the cabin's emergency lights turned off. "Let the soft rocking of the ship lull you into a gentle slumber..."

Holly shut her eyes but couldn't imagine ever falling asleep in such a terrifying racket. The shuttle shook like a wet dog trapped in a freezer. She was certain it would wrench itself apart at any moment. Yet soon she found her eyelids dropping lower and lower, and when she woke again they were less than five hours out from their destination.

Had she known what awaited them on Saturnalia, she would have taken the shuttle straight back.

CHAPTER
THREE

Carlson clung to the top of the ladder with his head poking through the hatch. With the shuttle no longer firing its thrusters and a period of weightlessness induced, his legs floated beneath him like a pair of foam pool noodles.

"No luck?" he asked the pilots.

Communication with Saturnalia was hardly an instantaneous exchange at the best of times. But even an hour away from docking, nobody at the station was answering any of the cockpit's frequent messages.

"Dammit. Comms are still out, then." He closed the latch behind him and climbed back down into the passenger cabin. "Well, s'pose we didn't make the trip for nothing. Strap in, guys. Deceleration's about to begin."

"Deceleration?" Holly whispered to Lynch.

"Can't apply the brakes in space," Banks answered from across the cabin. "The only way to slow down is to spin the shuttle around and accelerate in the opposite direction, cancelling out the original force."

"That doesn't sound fun," Holly replied.

"It's better than lift-off," Lynch said, pulling down her harness. "It's gradual, so you don't get the headaches half as bad."

"Hurts your butt, though," Wade added with a wicked smile.

Holly furrowed her brow.

"Why on earth would it hurt my—"

The thrusters roared to life and everyone who'd been happily floating an inch or two above their seat was slammed down into it. Holly let out a yelp as sharp pain ricocheted up her coccyx. She couldn't imagine how the boys felt.

"That's why," Lynch said with a wink.

"Watch yourself," Banks said. "Gravity's gonna get steadily weaker again the more we slow down."

Over the course of the following forty-five minutes – this time, Holly did keep track of them – the pressure on their bodies gradually lifted. Unfortunately, that wasn't the only thing that rose. Holly sensed a wet belch coming on, caught a stern look from Carlson, and just about kept the contents of her protein pouch down.

"Couldn't the company have forked out for a ship with artificial gravity?" she mumbled, her hand clasped over her mouth.

"Profit margins," Carlson grumbled with a subtle shake of his head. "It's all about those profit margins."

"I guess we're here, then. Stay in your seat," she said quickly, before Holly could excitedly release her harness. "If the station isn't answering, the pilots will have to dock manually."

"Is that a bad thing?"

"Not really." Banks managed to shrug in zero-G. "A delicate process, that's all."

"If Buzz Aldrin could do it over a hundred years ago," Wade said mockingly, "then I reckon the boys up top will be just fine."

Holly didn't think the comparison was entirely earned, but she took his point.

She thought she could hear the faint hiss of the air thrusters as the pilots carefully manipulated the shuttle into position. To think that Saturnalia was floating only a few metres from where she sat – from inside the cramped, windowless cabin, she could have just as easily been half a dozen lightyears away.

There was no imagining the sudden *clunk* as the shuttle attached itself to the station's airlock, however. It was followed by a long, awkward pause during which nobody inside the cabin said or did anything.

Then a green light switched on above the door through which they'd entered sixteen hours earlier and all the passengers hurriedly relieved themselves from their chairs.

Holly released her harness and undid her straps, then used them to pull herself over to the locker in which her few personal items were stashed. Three spare outfits, toiletries and, of course, the data pad with which she'd write her report. The lockers were padded so there was little chance anything in her bag had been damaged during the flight.

"Just the essentials for now," Carlson instructed the others. "We'll return for the rest of our gear, plus cargo, once we've ascertained the situation on the station."

"Yes, sir," Banks replied, handing out everybody's rifles.

With everybody floating in the centre of the cabin, seat-belts swaying around them like towers of kelp, Carlson punched a button that reminded Holly of the big red sort used to stop a factory's production line. The door hissed aside. Carlson reached out and, holding onto a bar beside the door with one hand, pulled each one of them through with the other.

Holly found herself drifting through the middle of a white, sterile corridor. Wade had to reach out and grab her before she smacked her face against the airlock door at the other end. Handholds scored the walls, floor and ceiling – not that she was entirely sure which was which. Lynch held down the button of a radio receiver.

"Saturnalia, this is a Flynn Industries security team. We were automatically dispatched following the comms blackout. Protocol 213. Permission to come aboard?"

Silence. She thumbed the button again.

"Saturnalia, do you read me?"

Lynch glanced over her shoulder and shook her head.

"Nobody's answering."

"If the comms issue stems from the core system rather than a malfunction of the array itself," Banks said calmly, "then it could be affecting the whole station, not just outgoing messages. I should be able to bypass the door controls from here."

"Without depressurising the docking tunnel?" Carlson asked.

"We've artificial atmospheres to either side of us," Banks replied, removing the safety panel. "Unless the Saturnalia's suffered a complete breach, we'll be fine."

Carlson raised his hand to his earpiece.

"Jones, Austin. You didn't pick up on any exterior damage to the station on your way in, did you?"

Everyone waited for the pilots' response.

"Didn't think so." Carlson nodded to Banks. "Okay. Go ahead."

Banks got to work. Holly couldn't tell if he was inputting an emergency access code or jerry-rigging the door open –

there were a lot of buttons and wires. All she knew was she didn't like the heavy feeling in her gut. Her report was already promising to look more like a damn novel.

The outer airlock doors hissed open. Everyone raised their rifles instinctively, but the airlock was just as unoccupied as the cabin of the shuttle behind them.

"All right," Carlson said. "Everyone inside. Lynch, make sure our analyst here doesn't fall flat on her face."

"Sorry, what?" Holly asked.

"You said you wanted artificial gravity," Lynch said, taking her by the arm. "You're gonna get it."

Banks gently swung himself into the airlock. The second he passed through the doors he plummeted towards the floor as if pulled by magnets. He stumbled forwards and made space for Wade, who repeated the motion.

"Your turn," Lynch said, placing Holly's hands on the bar overhead. "Don't float in head-first or you'll go arse over tit. Just imagine you're dropping down from a set of monkey bars. Actually, I'll push you."

Lynch gave Holly a friendly shove in the small of her back. Holly drifted forwards, hands and feet flailing rather pathetically, before crashing to the floor like a sack of potatoes. Banks reached out and caught her around the waist before she could drop to her knees. She let out a nervous laugh as she picked her bag up off the floor.

"Huh. Trippy."

"Boggles the mind, doesn't it?"

Lynch and Carlson followed with zero fanfare, then Banks input a code to cycle the airlock. The door behind them closed and vents hissed as chilly, moist air got pumped in. Holly wondered if they were being doused with disinfectant, too. Once the process was finished, the door ahead of them unlocked.

"Welcome to Saturnalia," Carlson grumbled to her as he marched past.

"Please wipe your feet," Wade added, flashing a semi-complete collection of mouth-stones the colour of dry wheat.

Holly gawped and gaped and was quite ready to believe this had all been a delirious hallucination brought on by a mass shift in cranial fluid upon take-off. Her eyes opened almost as wide as her mouth. She'd never in her life seen anywhere so fancy and knew, without so much as a shadow of doubt, never would again. A crystal chandelier more than half the size of their shuttle hung from the ceiling of a welcome lobby whose pillared walls had to be more than sixty feet in height. From its myriad tiers, orb-lamps glowed and candelabras flickered. Directly beneath it was an enormous reception desk built from deep, rich rosewood and polished brass. SATURNALIA was written beneath its counter and above the artificial waterfall behind in bold, art deco font. Twin grand staircases, carpeted in ruby red, curved around to either side of it towards an upper balcony that overlooked three available airlocks. The walls were panelled with more rosewood and brushed by the beams of spotlights hidden in alcoves, the floor tiled with marble, the ceiling designed to resemble that of a ballroom. Soft classical music was piped through air that smelled of sandalwood and vanilla.

It was a preposterously grandiose visitor's atrium for somewhere that welcomed notoriously few visitors, but she guessed there wasn't much point in being super-rich if those who weren't didn't know about it.

It was also extremely deserted.

"Huh." Wade looked put out. "Normally there's a welcome party."

"Well, without the comms array online," Lynch pointed out sarcastically, "there was no way to know we were coming..."

"They still would have been alerted when the ship docked," Carlson said sternly. His words echoed through the empty hall. "Eyes up, marines. Something ain't right."

Holly awkwardly cleared her throat.

"Should I head back to the shuttle, or...?"

"No, you'd best stick with us. Company'll want to know what's going on, specially if there *is* a problem. Just stay close and keep quiet."

"Security office is empty," Banks said, following a brief disappearance through an oak door on the left hand side of the atrium. "No sign of a struggle or anything. It's like the officers straight-up abandoned their post."

"Could be there's an issue requiring their attention elsewhere on the station," Carlson suggested. "Even so..."

He paused and turned back to the airlock with his finger pressed to his ear again.

"Pilots, you reading me okay? Good. Place is a damn ghost town. Nobody in sight. We're gonna push forward and investigate – don't let anyone on board the ship without my clearance, understand?"

"Or any*thing*," Wade joked under his breath.

"Focus, Wade. People could be hurt, or worse. And keep your fingers off those damn triggers, people. Nobody on my watch is blinding the first tycoon who comes running up to us for help. Now, move out."

With the atrium's offices already clear, the squad advanced towards the twin staircases. Lynch and Wade took the route on the right; Holly followed Carlson and Banks to the left. She could feel the plush carpet sighing beneath her shoes.

"At least we know the power's working," Lynch said as they climbed the steps. "That's something."

"And heating, and the air recycler," Banks added optimistically. "Whatever's gone on here, it doesn't seem to have affected core systems."

"Any way we can confirm that?" Carlson asked, glancing back down at the tranquil water feature.

"Sure, of course." Banks held the back of his hand against one of the grated vents running alongside the steps. "The monitor up in Administration will have all the station readouts. Or we could physically check out each component in Engineering."

"Then I reckon Administration's our first port of call," Carlson said, nodding. "Maybe Yang can explain what the hell's happening while we're at it."

Yang was a name Holly recognised. Andrew Yang was the administrator in charge of Saturnalia. In addition to the station's vital systems, he was responsible for monitoring workers, keeping the bars and kitchens stocked and communicating with Flynn Industries' headquarters back on New Terra. She was supposed to liaise with him upon arrival. Obviously he hadn't kept their appointment.

The balcony was no less lavish – greenery sprouted and cascaded from pots and planters along and up the walls, and rows of cushioned benches were set out like those of an old-fashioned train station. There was only one route forward, a spot-lit archway surrounded by oil portraits and sculptures on plinths.

"The founders of Saturnalia," Banks said, noticing Holly's gaze. "Yeah, it doesn't get any less pretentious from here on out..."

"That one's Old Mr. Flynn," Lynch said quietly, nodding

to a bust just to the right of the entranceway. "I'm guessing a little corporate hotshot like you's interested."

Holly couldn't see the resemblance, but then it wasn't as if she spent her nights studying pictures of the late Albert Flynn anyway. He looked like any old, over-moustached white guy to her, albeit one who'd had his head caked in gold. Never the type to keep up with business or finance outside of work, she doubted she'd have any better luck identifying the rest of the founders either.

The corridor beyond was wide, open, ringed with brass and round like a tunnel in an aquarium. At the far end were the façades of what looked like Parisian shops from a hundred years ago or more. Holly supposed the architect had intended the walkway to generate excitement and anticipation in new arrivals, but the only thing she felt building as it went on was nausea. And not because of the space travel this time. Something about the silence was very, very wrong.

Because it wasn't quite silence, was it? Even putting aside the echoing footsteps and the ambient hum of electrics and the gentle tinkling of ivory keys, there was something else lurking on the periphery, scratching to get in like a secret you didn't want whispered in your ear.

All four ex-marines jerked their rifles up as an equal number of men and women sprinted around the corner. Their suits and dresses had been reduced to rags. The women's greasy hair had tumbled loose from their buns. Their hands and distraught faces were stained with dry blood.

Carlson lowered his rifle first, gestured for the others to do the same.

"At ease. They're just residents." He nodded to them. "Hey, slow down. We're from the company. Can any of you tell me what's going on here?"

"Thank g-goodness somebody came," the waistcoated man at the front spluttered. "We tried c-calling for help, b-but..."

"They've all gone quite mad," a woman in a tattered black cocktail dress said frantically. "They tried to destroy it, would you believe?"

"You're safe now," Carlson said as the group drew level with them. "Take a moment. Breathe. Explain what happened."

"Everything was p-perfect," said the man in the dirty waistcoat. "But some of them, they w-wouldn't listen, they couldn't *see*, and the t-truth... the truth, it's for only a certain k-kind of person, you see, and... a-and—"

"We need to locate Dr. Humphreys," Carlson whispered urgently to Banks. "They've clearly experienced some kind of traumatic event."

The resident's mask slipped and his stutter vanished with it.

"—and I suppose you could say we're not accepting visitors this present moment."

The man swung a piece of broken pipe and cracked it against Carlson's skull. The ex-marine collapsed in a jerky fit, foam spilling from his mouth.

"Shit!" Lynch shot the man as he raised the pipe to bludgeon Carlson a second time. "Get Bloom back to the ship, now—"

The woman in the cocktail dress pulled out a steak knife from behind her back and plunged it into Lynch's neck. Dark blood sprayed across the sleek alabaster floor. Lynch dropped her rifle and grasped, wide eyed and open mouthed, for the weapon still sticking from her jugular. More blood gushed between her fingers, and she collapsed to the ground with the knife still lodged up to its hilt.

Wade shot the woman in the face. The rubber bullet destroyed most of her jaw, teeth scattering like red and white marbles. She screamed and clutched at her mouth, writhing on the floor while the other two residents finished clubbing the inert Carlson to death.

Banks grabbed Holly's arm and dragged her back towards the shuttle. She remembered hearing somebody shriek when Carlson had first been hit, and had a horrid suspicion the sound had come from her own mouth. This was all happening to somebody else far from here, like she was watching events unfold through a virtual reality sim. Cold, heavy numbness. She felt as dead a weight in Banks's arm as the golden busts standing watch outside the corridor.

"This place is a fuckin' horror show," Wade shouted, backing up alongside them. He kept firing at the residents. None were dead – yet – but neither were they in any hurry to get back up.

"Let the company sort this mess out," Banks replied. "They can send in a proper strike team. Or just nuke the bastards for all I care."

"Lynch, dude. *Shit*. Carlson, too."

"I know, man. I know."

They were back onto the atrium's balcony when Banks abruptly stopped. Holly almost barrelled right past him, her legs had grown so heavy. With Wade no longer firing his rifle, one sound suddenly stood out amongst the cries and groans.

Footsteps rushing up the stairs ahead of them.

"Where the hell are they even coming from?" Banks grunted, reluctantly pulling Holly back inside the connecting corridor.

"I'll hold 'em off," Wade shouted, advancing towards the steps. "Get her somewhere safe."

But Banks had nowhere left to go. Some of the attackers Wade had wounded were climbing back to their feet, clasping their bruised ribs, and even more psychos spilled out from deeper inside the station behind them.

Holly looked up into Banks's astonished face.

"I... I don't want to die here..." she babbled, breaking free from the shock. "Why did I think this was... Oh God..."

He cast his eyes down at her, turned his attention back to the madmen rushing down the tunnel towards them, and then let go of her arm. There was a vent belching out warm air to the left of them. He smashed its grate with the butt of his rifle until the bolts gave out and it collapsed inwards.

"Get in," he shouted. "Go on, go!"

Holly dropped to her hands and knees and crawled inside. It was a tight fit. Only once she was a few metres down did she realise she'd dropped her bag somewhere in the panic.

It was dark. She tried to turn around, found there wasn't room, and settled for craning her head against the top of the grimy vent instead. The warm and dusty air choked her lungs. The tiny square of light behind her flickered as angry boots crossed back and forth.

She flinched at the sound of a rifle being fired over and over, cowered as Banks shouted for people to stay back, *pleaded* with them, winced as the screams and cries and groans from the citizens of Saturnalia grew louder. And then, suddenly, silence.

Holly dared to inch back outside.

Banks's face crashed to the floor outside the vent's opening, his eyes glassy and a steady trickle of blood descending from his temple. *Stay where you are*, he almost seemed to be saying to her. *Don't move*. So she didn't. She kept still, her hand clasped tightly over her mouth to stifle her screams, as residents stalked the halls in search of survivors.

Eventually, even the last set of footsteps faded away.

And still she waited, tears streaming silently down her face as she broke eye-contact with the deceased and dared to crawl deeper into the pitch-black belly of the space station.

Screw the report, she decided. Priority One was escaping Saturnalia with her life.

Holly didn't know how long she crawled for, only that the further she descended the warmer the metal beneath her hands became. More than once she had to take pause while her lungs coughed up the latest batch of stale dust she'd inhaled.

All of this in pitch-blackness, scrambling blindly, slipping on grease and oil, tumbling down ducts and hitting her head on sharp corners.

In constant dread that the security team's murderers could hear her.

Her heart fluttered when she suddenly realised she could make out the rusty bolts holding the sections of her ventilation shaft together and the dark, damp patches that squelched under her fingers. It wasn't a bright light that emanated from around the next corner, but in the darkness it was as comforting a beacon as that of a lighthouse.

Of course, lighthouses were built to keep sailors from dashing their boats against the rocks, but in lieu of any other path through the darkness Holly felt she had no choice but to push towards it and hope for better fortune.

The light came from another grate, less intricate than the one through which she first crawled and this time embedded in the floor of the shaft. Holding her breath, she peered down at the room below. Her hair fell past her face and through the gaps, blocking her view; she frustratedly wrapped the loose strands around her fingers and tried again.

The angle of the vent didn't give her much in the way of perspective, no matter how close she brought her face to the dust-lined slats. It looked like a small room below her. Some kind of office or storage closet. A desk or workbench, some shelves, the bottom of what she believed to be a closed door. There was no way of knowing whether the room continued much further behind the vent, but given the narrowness of what little Holly could see, she highly doubted it.

As she pulled her face away, she noticed that the duct continued on beyond the grate quite some distance; far enough, in fact, that it once more disappeared into blind darkness.

She could keep going, see where else she ended up – if anywhere. But sooner or later she'd have to leave the vent. It wasn't as if she could crawl her way back to New Terra. Better to exit while she could before she fell down a dead-end shaft from which she couldn't climb back out.

Her nose tickled. She stifled a sneeze. It probably wouldn't have mattered, anyway – through the closed door below Holly thought she could hear the whirs, grunts and chugs of heavy machinery. Still, it presented an interesting dilemma. How was she supposed to escape this aluminium prison without the psychopaths upstairs hearing her?

She tried to find screws to undo, but they were all on the outside of the vent and her fingers weren't long or dextrous enough to reach them through the slats. Neither were there any latches. She guessed the vents hadn't been designed with inner-station transit in mind.

Holly remembered how Banks had smashed the previous grate open with the butt of his rifle. That grate had looked sturdier, too, though Banks was also quite a few magnitudes stronger than her. Well, he had been. And she didn't have a gun, unfortunately, though she did possess a pair of legs that hadn't been completely reduced to rubber by her sixteen hour spaceflight.

It was a painful procedure, but Holly managed to squeeze herself around inside the vent so that her head pointed back the way she came. Thank God she'd chosen practical work shoes for the trip. She went to boot the grate with both feet, then hesitated.

What was her plan if the psychos *did* come running?

"Even if they are down there, I'll still be up here," she whispered to herself unconvincingly.

Yeah. Stuck in an air duct with nowhere else to go, you idiot. They won't need to catch you, just starve you out.

Well, she was dead if she hid up there forever anyway.

Holly booted the grate once, then waited. Nobody came. Then she booted it again, and still nothing. One of the screws had come loose, though – she could see a tiny strip of light poking through the top-right corner. A third kick and the top half of the grate broke free completely, dangling from its two remaining screws before crashing catastrophically into the room below.

She scuttled backwards on her rear and shut her eyes tight, like a child playing hide-and-seek who thinks if they can't see the hunter, the hunter can't see them either. But there came no cries of triumphant murderers, no smashing in of closet doors, no furious scrabbling to climb inside her vent. After a minute or more passed, Holly dared believe her escape had gone unnoticed.

Or it was some kind of trap... but if that was the case, she had no choice left but to spring it.

Unwilling to turn around in the vent again, and not exactly excited by the idea of plunging into the room head-first, Holly slowly inched her legs out over the hole in the vent until she was sitting on the edge – or would have been, had she the headroom to sit upright. She flipped herself onto her front, her legs kicking at empty air, and tried to lower herself down gently... only to remember too late that she had nothing inside the vent to hold onto.

Grasping impotently at every passing panel of the duct, she felt the edge of the grate's frame run up her belly and over her chest. A sharp pain shot up her arm as she finally fell free.

She landed on the hard floor and rolled about clutching her tailbone. She'd be lucky to only get a bad bruise, the way it ached. Then, forgetting the pain for a moment, she scrambled backwards and cowered in the corner furthest from the door with her arms wrapped over her knees.

It didn't open.

She was okay. Hurt, but okay.

"No, you're not," she whispered to herself. "You're trapped on board a space station full of maniacs who've killed your security escort and probably want you dead, too. And you're lost. You are far from fucking okay, Holly."

She looked down at her shirt. If it wasn't bad enough that each inch of her clothing was now dirtier than a dishrag, it was also covered in blood. Fresh blood.

"Oh, shit."

Slipping out of the vent had carved a gash up her left arm. Fortunately, it wasn't deep, and the bleeding had already reduced to a trickle. A scratch with gory aspirations. But an out-of-control satellite above Saturn was hardly somewhere you wanted to contract an infection. If the doctor on Saturnalia was as mad as the rest of the residents she'd encountered so far, there might not be a qualified medical professional for lightyears. It needed dressing.

She rose to her feet, holding her arm out to keep it from rubbing against her filthy clothes. Drops of blood peppered the concrete floor. The room was as she expected – a glorified broom closet full of spare supplies. A set of literal brooms, buckets and mops were stashed in a corner close to the door, and the floor to ceiling shelves were stocked with everything from oil canisters to wire coils to bottled water. A cluttered desk stood to one side. A single dim lightbulb hung by its wire from the middle of the ceiling.

Rummaging through the shelves and pulling open drawers at random, she found a collection of oily rags stashed inside the desk. One towards the back looked comparatively unused. She grabbed one of the bottles of water and poured it first over the wound and then the rag before guzzling what remained. Then she took the rag and wrapped it tightly around her arm.

Holly examined her handiwork. It was a poor substitute for gauze, but it would do for now.

She sat on the edge of the desk and caught her breath. Great job, Holly. She ran her hands down her face, stopped with them clasped over her mouth in exasperation and disbelief. Really great job. Half a decade this space station's been floating above Saturn problem-free, and by the time you get to it all hell's broken loose.

"Christ, Holly." She felt like crying, like screaming, like smashing everything in the storage room to pieces. "Why the hell did you volunteer for this?"

But she knew why, even if she couldn't let on to her supervisor or the security team. And perhaps this was exactly the reason she needed to come here in the first place. Bad timing, that's all.

Really bad timing.

"Pull yourself together," she told herself. "You don't get paid enough to be slaughtered by a bunch of billionaires with cabin fever. Even if some of those billionaires are the ones who sign your payslips..."

She turned around, pressed her hands against the desk instead. A complicated map of Saturnalia was fastened to the wall above it, and stuck around its frame were all manner of notes and lists scribbled on recycled paper that had been over-pulped almost to the point of being mulch. The notes Holly didn't care about, and the map was too full of annotations and cross-sections and mechanical diagrams for a layperson like herself to follow. But this was her first chance to study the station's basic structure. The plans to Saturnalia simply weren't available to outsiders, not even Flynn Industries employees.

"So I'm guessing I've ended up somewhere in here," she said, tracing the part of the map marked *Engineering*. It sure sounded like that's where she was, anyway. "And the shuttle is all the way back up here, outside the atrium of the section marked *Residential District*."

Dammit. The atrium was two whole sections away. *Engineering, Workers' District, Residential District.* And who even knew how many subfloors divided each. This little stowaway rat *had* scurried far, hadn't she?

There. She tapped the map with her finger. It wasn't labelled, but it *looked* as if there was a large elevator connecting the bottom two sectors, if not the third as well.

Of course, that meant missing out on visiting the top two

tiers of the station – *Resort District* and *Operations & Observation* – but something told her they wouldn't be quite as much fun as they sounded anymore.

All she had to do was get back up to the Residential District and sneak through the welcome lobby to the shuttle without anyone seeing her, and maybe she could get off this station alive.

Piece of cake, right?

Holly sucked her teeth. She hadn't been able to sneak back inside her parents' apartment on Earth as a teenager without waking them. Not even when she'd been sober, which admittedly hadn't been too often. It wasn't as if she'd garnered much experience of espionage and subterfuge since.

Well, it's that or die in a broom closet. Yes, it's a stellar upgrade from the ventilation system, but still.

She tightened the makeshift bandage on her arm and paused beside the door, listening for footsteps.

Oh God, she thought, her hand shaking on the brass handle. What if it's locked? To get back into that vent I'd need to climb up the bloody shelves. And even then...

But the handle turned, the bolt slid free, and the door creaked slowly open. The closet was suddenly filled with the roar of angry machinery.

She inhaled sharply as she summoned the nerve to leave.

"Welcome to Saturnalia, indeed."

CHAPTER
FIVE

Yeah, she was down in Engineering all right.

It was like walking into a grinder. She wished there'd been a pair of ear protectors inside that broom closet. Instead she had to cover both her ears with her hands, which was sure to make the sight of her crouching around the machinery all the more laughable. One silver lining was that nobody else would hear her skulking about, she supposed.

Then again, she wouldn't hear them, either.

Every inch of space was dedicated either to giant machinery or the multi-tiered gangways that encircled them. Not that she could identify anything by model, but the water reclaimer, boilers, atmospheric synthesiser and electric generators all had to be down here. And boy, was it as hot as it was noisy. Sweat dripping off your forehead, panting like a dog *hot*. No wonder the vents ran all the way from Engineering to the upper levels. The excess heat alone was enough to keep the VIPs from freezing all the way up on their Mount Olympus.

That there weren't any workers tending to the equipment hardly came as a surprise. If the people on the floor above her at Flynn Industries ever went homicidal, Holly probably wouldn't bother coming into the office either.

Of course, that raised an interesting question. If the workers weren't here, where *had* they all got to?

Eh. That was a problem for the workers to worry about, she guessed.

Holly left the comparative safety of her broom closet door and crept forward between a pair of giant belching, chugging pistons. She could just about hear the rattling of the diamond-treaded sheet of metal beneath her feet, of the bolts and screws shaking themselves loose. Leaning over the railing, she noticed another network of gangways mirroring hers below and possibly, if the shimmering heat haze didn't deceive her squinting eyes, yet another lattice further below that. Thick pipes, streaked with rust after only five or six years of operation, ran overhead, split apart, and dived into various machineries. Fat, insulated electrical cables were clipped to their length and the fluorescent light strips hanging from the ceiling weren't in much better condition than the dim lone bulb Holly had encountered earlier.

A far cry from the world above, but Holly supposed those who funded Saturnalia didn't exactly frequent the lower levels so much as actively avoid them.

"You'd think they'd spring for a few goddamn signs, though," she muttered to herself. "How the hell is anyone supposed to find their way around this place?"

She encountered a stairwell leading to the platforms below but continued past it – if anything she needed to be heading upwards, not down. She risked walking less like a hunchback, too – Engineering appeared utterly abandoned.

A giant immersion heater shaped like a sea mine designed to destroy submarines hissed and shook from mounting pressure. Maybe that's how it was supposed to work, but without regular maintenance it wouldn't be long before the heart of Saturnalia broke apart and its lifeblood stopped pumping.

Now, Holly was no expert, but it didn't seem wise to still be on the cold, airless space station caught in a decaying orbit around an inhospitable gas giant when that happened.

If only the damn map had sported a "You Are Here" sticker. She had no way of knowing whether she was headed towards the maintenance elevator or away from it. She needed a tour guide or a NavMap, or something. If she carried on like this, she'd be stuck wandering the industrial labyrinth for hours.

She turned the corner and shrieked.

A member of the Engineering team stood before her. Well, he didn't stand, exactly. The tips of his reinforced boots may have brushed the floor of the hanging walkway, but he was only held upright by the three steel rods pinning him to the adjacent pillar. Each was impaled through his rib cage. His dented yellow hard hat hung off one of their ends.

The word *traitor* was scrawled across the pillar in the victim's blood.

Holly spun around and resisted the urge to throw up. She kept her hand clasped over her mouth for much longer than it took her stomach to settle again. The machinery surrounding her was loud, but her cry had been even louder – not to mention considerably higher in pitch. Maybe anyone looking for her could have mistaken it for a whistle of steam, but—

She dropped to her knees. A flicker of shadow on the catwalk below, she was sure of it. Maybe it belonged to a piston, or a bunch of flailing wires that had broken loose, or maybe it was just a trick of the light or her rapidly unravelling mind. But the only sensible response was to assume it was somebody on the hunt for her. Somebody who saw her crawl into the vent and knew where she'd be forced to crawl back out.

Shit. She couldn't stay put – sooner or later, they'd find her. But moving was just as stupid an idea if she didn't know where she was going.

Maybe she should have grabbed Banks's gun when he collapsed outside her vent. It would have fallen within reach. But then the residents would have probably found and killed her, too. And it wasn't as if she'd ever fired a weapon before in her life. In fact, she didn't think she'd ever wielded anything more dangerous than a wrench, back when she helped her dad fix the leak under their bathroom sink.

Stop being so stupid, she told herself. If a security team formed of ex-marines couldn't survive, what chance do you think *you* have?

Yeah, but you've got one advantage the others didn't. *You* know everyone on the station is dangerous. So whatever else you do, stay the hell out of sight.

And if you can't do that, run.

Another glance at the man hanging from the pillar convinced her to keep moving. Not past him, mind you. Instead, she crouched her way along a longer, rickety bridge that ran perpendicular to her original path, praying that each step didn't rattle its metal floor like a tinny alarm bell, wishing that the light in her new subterranean world wasn't so coppery and its jagged shadows quite so deep.

As she passed over a gigantic vat of water occupying most of the following hall, she started to suspect that any maintenance elevator would be found down on the ground floor – presuming she ever *did* find it, that is – rather than up in the rafters. She hadn't spotted a single doorway or other such exit since abandoning the closet, only odd nooks and alcoves full of pipes and cranks and circuit breakers. The next time she came across a staircase to the level below, she took it, hid on the steps while anxiously scrutinising the crowded machinery for any more suspicious movement, and then hurriedly followed it the rest of the way to the bottom.

The dusty, oily concrete beneath her shoes made her feel sturdier, like a seasick passenger finally setting foot on dry land again, and less exposed. The tapping of her shoes wasn't nearly as bad as their clanging against the metal, and she no longer needed to worry about poorly maintained architecture giving her position away. The water storage vat – it had to be even greater in volume than an Olympic swimming pool – was surrounded on all sides by smaller tanks, each accompanied by its own array of valves and pressure gauges, and she quickly took cover behind the nearest set.

"Come on out of your hidey-hole, darlings," said a voice like champagne served in a sandpaper flute, just as she scampered into position. "We know you're still down here."

Holly froze mid-breath. Her heart hammered so hard it actually hurt, and her pounding temples distracted eyes that already stung from all the sweat running into them.

Dammit. They must have spotted her coming down the steps.

She clenched her fists hard enough for her nails to impress little crescent moons in the flesh of her palms. She scrunched her eyes shut tight, then forced herself to keep them open. It was okay to be scared, she told herself, but not to give up.

"Don't be afraid," the man cried out in his shrill, raspy voice. "You've nothing to fear from the truth."

Holly had seen their truth, and it arrived on the sharp end of steak knives and broken pipes. She carefully peered around the console behind which she'd crouched. The man stalked the underside of the lowest gallery about twenty-five, maybe thirty metres from her position. He had a tall, wire-frame physique which only grew more unsettling as it contorted in the heat haze. The sleeves of his expensive khaki-coloured shirt were rolled up to the elbows. Judging by the state of his floppy hair and overgrown stubble, the grinning man hadn't showered or slept in days.

He changed direction and Holly shot back into cover.

Darlings. Plural. An odd turn of phrase unless he really thought there were others hiding down here. Had Wade somehow survived the attack in the atrium and followed her through the vents?

But he'd also said *we*, hadn't he? She knew that the upper echelons of society sometimes used the *royal 'we'* in place of personal pronouns, but still...

Slowly, stepping so gently that her shoes didn't even tap against the concrete, Holly crept towards the next tank over. The man didn't appear to know where she was. It was unfortunate, then, that she didn't know where she was either. She reached the tank and nestled herself amongst the intricate lattice of cold pipes.

The man had come from the other direction, ahead of where she now hid. She had to assume he wasn't living down here amongst all the noise and heat. And how else would he have followed her to Engineering if not via the maintenance elevator? Even if she'd misread the schematics, surely he'd taken a stairwell or some other form of lift that would lead back to the upper sectors.

Wiping a fresh film of sweat off her lip with the back of her hand – and wincing as the searing pain from the cut under her bandage – Holly inched back out of her hiding space... and then almost cracked her head against a wheel-valve as she doubled back.

Yeah, the crazy man was most definitely *not* alone.

Two more psychos had joined him – an Asian gentleman sporting a preposterously manicured quiff and a woman whose dirty night-frock made her look more Victorian gutter-rat than high-class aristocracy. They prowled as hyenas, their wide, bloodshot eyes underscored with dark rings and twitching from shadow to shadow. The woman appeared to be carrying a walking stick, its end sharpened to a splintered point.

Holly chewed her lip and tried to ignore the way her trembling legs threatened to collapse under her. So much for that plan, then. They had every angle covered except back up the steps behind her, and even if she could make it halfway up before they noticed her, then what? It wasn't as if she could outrun them if she didn't even know where to run *to*.

She jumped as the woman let out a mad cackling sound and smacked the cane against one of the water tanks. They were closing in. She imagined being impaled against the wall with the walking stick like that poor engineer and let out an involuntary whimper.

She raised her hand to her mouth, felt her fingers brush away tears she hadn't realised she'd been crying.

Well, Holly, they haven't caught you yet.

She took a slow, tentative step backwards while facing the three probing maniacs, then another, and then another, all the while ready to spin around and leg it up the rickety metal staircase the second they inevitably noticed her.

Almost there... Almost there...

Suddenly, a rough, foul-smelling hand clasped her

mouth shut from behind. A second arm wrapped around her middle and squeezed tight. She tried breaking free but would have had better luck escaping a strait jacket.

They dragged her kicking, if not screaming, back into the belly of the big brass beast.

CHAPTER SIX

Holly's shoes skimmed and scraped the floor as she was dragged behind rows of tall copper cylinders and steel girders. She couldn't open her mouth wide enough to bite the man's hand, and she couldn't swing her one free arm around far enough to land a proper hit. A pair of short, triangular walls crept past and then suddenly she was thrown through a small hole into a cramped, foul-smelling room full of blankets and buckets.

She spun around ready to scratch her mystery assailant's eyes out, but when he turned back to her after sliding a sheet of corrugated tin across the room's opening, they looked just as wide and frightened as hers.

"What the f—"

"They'll hear you," he whispered, desperately waving his hands back and forth.

The man grabbed Holly's shoulder and pulled her down into a crouched position beside the tin sheet. She shrugged him off with a scowl, but he only replied by raising a finger to his lips and gesturing madly at the world outside.

She bit her lip and listened.

Nothing at first, save for the ever-present ambience of ear-piercing pump-work. And then footsteps. Loud, confident footsteps that didn't mind being heard. They stopped close by. Holly shuddered as something heavy thudded into the ground a moment later.

"Those who are naughty," a male voice said sweetly, "tend to get caughty..."

There was a harsh metallic scraping sound and then the footsteps moved further away. About half a minute later, Holly's captor visibly deflated with relief.

"I think they're gone—"

"Who the hell are you?" Holly spat, shoving the man over. "And what do you think you're doing, grabbing me like that?"

"Saving you, of course!" The man rubbed his bruised backside. "Or did you want those freaks to feed you into the grinder?"

Holly didn't know what Engineering's grinder was for, but no, she didn't much like the sound of being its next meal. She shook her head in frustration and examined her enclosure. There was scarcely room for either of them to stand up straight. Hell, there was scarcely enough floor space for them to stand at all. Every inch was covered in oily rags and towels, or upturned buckets, or piles of ration pouches and water bottles. Evidently, this was some kind of hideout. Lights on the dark grey wall blinked on and off like an orderly spreadsheet of stars.

The man stood up and extended a nervous hand.

"I'm Fritz, by the way. Fritz Fredersen."

Holly studied the greasy mitt on offer, then decided to shake it. Hopefully this Fritz guy hadn't gone to all the trouble of saving her life just so he could end it himself.

"Holly Bloom. What is this place?"

"It's the servers for the hydro-generator," Fritz explained. "That's, erm... that's why it's a bit cooler, see? They'd overheat if they were kept outside with everything else."

"Sure." She could feel a breeze from small fans set into the ceiling. "Makes sense."

"Most of the maintenance team probably didn't know about this spot," Fritz continued, scratching behind his ear. "More mechanical engineers down here than electrical. I'm hoping that's why nobody's found me yet. You're not from Saturnalia, are you?"

"No. Came here with a security team when station comms went dark. They're all dead."

"So you have a ship, right? A way off?"

Holly laughed dryly.

"Yeah, I'm working on that. Like I said, the team's dead. For all I know the pilots are, too. Either way, I've got to survive my trip back to the shuttle first. What the fuck happened here, Fritz?"

The engineer shrugged defeatedly.

"Who knows, lady."

"Come on, man." Holly gestured to the messy hideout. "You got somewhere better to be, or something? Spill."

Fritz sighed and collapsed onto a pile of rags he likely used as a bed... presuming the man had gotten any sleep at all.

"I mean, I can tell you what I heard. I'm no expert, that's all. Pull up a pew."

One of the buckets had a thick rag draped over it like a cushion. Holly pulled it over. It sloshed.

"Oh, I, erm, wouldn't sit there. I haven't been using that one as a chair, so to speak."

"Ah." Holly winced. "Gotcha."

Pulling over a more suitable seat, Holly got her first

chance to take Fritz in without the threat of imminent murder hanging over them. Despite having overcome her so easily, he wasn't a large man. He still wore his blue engineer's uniform, though his sleeves were rolled up to reveal a mishmash of faded tattoos. She would have described his face as almost gaunt, and it was etched with enough worry lines that she estimated he was in his late forties, early fifties. Of course, the last few days could have aged the poor, German-accented man considerably – if life working in the underbelly of Saturnalia hadn't done so already.

"Like I said, rumours are all I've got." Fritz shrugged. "You hear one thing from someone working in the suites, then something else altogether from your mate in warehousing, and then before you know it the whole station's *kaputt*. You may as well be asking me how the carbon scrubbers work."

"Aren't you an engineer?"

"Not that kind. Anyway, let's see. Tuesday, I think it was – that's when it started. Or was it Monday? It's hard to tell without a day-night cycle. The morning began the same as always – bells went off for shift change, so Maria and I got dressed and went down for breakfast—"

"I'm sorry," Holly said. "Did you say the *bells* went off? What is this, the schoolyard?"

"They have to keep a tight ship on the Saturnalia," Fritz replied, shrugging embarrassedly. "Lives are at stake if something goes wrong, you know? Bells, breakfast, bathroom. Always in that order. Wake up at five a.m. station time, start our shift at six. Keeps everything running as it's s'posed to, and if someone's sick, Mr. Velasquez knows who needs covering what."

Holly shook her head in disbelief.

"Yeah, whatever. Sorry for interrupting. Carry on."

"So anyway – everything was the same as always, right down to the porridge they served in the canteen that morning. I went to work on the hydro-generator – they needed to divert a little extra juice to Operations, I remember. An EVA pod had been deployed for routine maintenance a day or two before, and as a result the docking bay's chargers needed a boost in power. And I think Madame Gosselin was planning to put on a matinee show in the Resort District that afternoon. Nobody was saying or doing anything out of the ordinary, I swear. Like I said, everything ticked along like clockwork.

"That changed after lunch, I guess. Maybe it was something in the sandwiches, you know?" Fritz smiled sheepishly to show this was a joke. "Violence broke out in the Residential District. I heard people say that one of the older gentlemen slapped a maid for misplacing a hairbrush or something, and maybe that's true. But I was also told that all the staff up there suddenly stopped what they were doing and tried to take over the station. I don't know who to believe. Sure, people weren't exactly happy with how things were run here, but... oh, whatever. Maybe it's all true, maybe none of it is. But once word of the attack spread down here, everyone wanted a piece of it. Only a few of us stayed behind to make sure the core systems didn't go offline, and nobody came back. Well, nobody came back the way they left, at least."

Holly chewed her bottom lip.

"So, what? This is some kind of revolution gone wrong, is that what you're saying? That the workers took up arms against the rich and now all the survivors have gone mad with bloodlust?"

"You tell me, lady." Fritz shrugged. "I've been hiding down here ever since."

"And it's just you? There's nobody else down here? I ran into another engineer on the upper galleries. He was, erm, looking a little worse for wear."

Fritz shuddered.

"Yes, that was Mikhailov. A good man. I gather he came down here to sabotage the boilers so they would blow, but I can't imagine why. How would that help the workers *or* the residents? Either way, we'd all die."

Holly froze.

"Did *you* stop him?" she asked, slowly reaching down to grab her bucket for use as a weapon.

"What? No!" Fritz was aghast. "I tried to take his body down the last time I dared leave this place. I hate knowing he's up there on display. But I couldn't bring myself to handle all that, well, blood."

"All right." Holly relaxed slightly. "Well, I don't blame you for—"

A loud bang went off back near the water tanks. They jumped and watched the makeshift door in fear.

"Probably just a pipe cooling," Fritz whispered. "Won't be long before stuff breaks and we all suffocate or freeze to death."

"And what was your plan before I came along? To sit here feeling sorry for yourself until that happened?"

"What else do you expect me to do?" he hissed. "Until *you* came along, everyone else on Saturnalia was either dead or insane! So you *do* have a plan to escape, then?"

"I told you, I'm working on it. I'm an analyst, for crying out loud – I'm probably less equipped to deal with an outbreak of station-wide psychosis than you are. At least you know how to swing a wrench, right?" Holly nodded brusquely. "What about that Maria woman you mentioned?"

"What about her?"

"The two of you are obviously close. You woke up together, and I'm guessing that's not because you're bunk mates. Where's she?"

Fritz bowed his head.

"Maria's my wife. Been married nineteen years, since before the Exodus. Agreeing to work in this damn place was our only ticket off Earth, you understand. She works as a housekeeper in the suites. Each morning I go down, and she goes up."

"And... she's not down here with you."

"No, she isn't. Maria would have been in the suites when it all happened. If she wasn't caught up in the madness, she might have tried getting back to our quarters, but..."

"So what are you sitting around here for?" Holly tried rousing him to his feet. "She could be hiding somewhere upstairs worrying about *you!* You have to go find her."

"Why?" Fritz raised his head; his voice rose with it. "She's dead, isn't she? Everybody's fucking dead!"

"Okay, okay." Holly hurriedly quieted him. Too far. She'd pushed too far. "But you don't know for sure. You survived, and I'm sure she's just as capable, right? Don't give up hope. I don't think either of us can afford to do that right now."

She pointed at Fritz's cache of food.

"Do you mind? I haven't eaten since before my shuttle docked. I'm starving."

"Help yourself," he replied, sagging. "I just grabbed everything I could from Velasquez's office when workers stopped coming back. I can't imagine I'll be alive long enough to eat it all, anyway."

Holly grabbed a protein bar at random and unwrapped it with shaking fingers. Her head and stomach were beginning to ache again. Taking a bite, she wasn't entirely sure what flavour the bar was supposed to be – if they even bothered putting flavouring into food destined for the lower levels, that is. Something akin to salted chicken, perhaps.

"Look, I'm going to let you in on a secret," she said between mouthfuls. "I *am* an analyst, and I *was* sent by the company to assess the damage to your comm array, run costs, etcetera. But that's not the real reason I came here. Quite frankly, I couldn't give two shits whether the company can chat with its shareholders or not. I was sent to find Rosie Flynn. You know, the wife of Lewis Flynn?"

"Yeah, I've heard of her," Fritz replied. His eyes suddenly grew wide. "Wait. She must have known something was about to happen on the station and requested urgent retrieval before this comms blackout you mentioned. That's it, right? Whatever erupted upstairs must have been brewing for days. God, I bet her bastard husband is behind all this somehow. He's always hated us blue-collars."

Holly awkwardly swallowed another chunk of protein bar.

"Sure. Probably." She waved her wrapper dismissively. "All I know is she needs finding now worse than ever. Maybe she's dead already. Maybe she's gone as mad as all the rest. But if she doesn't take a swing at me, I'm sure as hell getting her off Saturnalia."

"You'd risk your life to save a Flynn? Do you really care that much about the company?"

"Hell, no. I care that much about *me*. Consider Rosie Flynn to be my ticket to a better life."

It was Fritz's turn to look at Holly as if she were the threat.

"You won't survive five minutes out there on your own. If it weren't for me, those loonies would have bludgeoned your brains out already."

"Now you're getting it." Holly tossed the empty wrapper to one side and leaned close. "I need a guide. An escort. Someone who knows his way around the guts of this station. Help me find this woman and I'll make sure you get off safely, too."

Fritz stared at her, then buried his head in his hands.

"Maria's gone. Deep in my heart, I know that. I've always been a pessimist, and God, I don't see how the past few days should change anything. But Maria – she wouldn't want me to die in a hole like this."

He's a coward, Holly thought. But he's not wrong.

"I don't care about the Flynns," he said, climbing to his feet. "I think you should leave them to rot in this horrid place. But I reckon I can get us back up to that shuttle of yours, if it's still waiting. If after that you want to die chasing ghosts, that's up to you."

"Seems fair enough," she replied, trying not to show her relief. "So, how are we doing this? I think I saw a maintenance elevator on the floor plan."

Fritz crossed to the tin sheet and peered through a tiny crack separating it from the frame of the small opening behind.

"Yeah, you did. We'll wait until they're definitely gone," he said without peeling his eye from the slit. "Then we'll stick to the pipe-walls round back. It takes longer, but it's safer."

She impatiently flexed her palms open and closed.

"Sure. Works for me. Can't find anyone if we're dead."

Holly tried to make herself comfortable on her bucket. So she'd found herself a guide. Good. No more stumbling around terrified in the dark.

Now all she needed to do was figure out an actual escape plan before she got them both killed.

CHAPTER
SEVEN

They waited almost twenty minutes before Fritz felt comfortable enough to slide the tin sheet away from the opening and let Holly crawl through. She was blown away by how much fresher the air tasted outside the hideout despite its hot, weighty undertones of iron and petroleum.

Fritz frantically returned the sheet to its original position, then cowered in the shadow of the hydro-generator's triangular support strut. Holly shook him by the shoulder.

"Which way?" she hissed.

He scoured the interlocking maze of pipes, pumps and pillars with a pair of eyes like runny eggs, then finally jabbed his thumb over his shoulder.

"Follow me."

He sprinted around the strut, hunched so low his knees were practically playing his ribcage like a glockenspiel, and weaved between the pillars and gantry girders like a skier through slalom gates. Holly tried her best to keep up with him, her gut squeezing every time she stepped out into the open, resisting the urge to stop and hide between each support in case she lost sight of her escort. She suspected she couldn't even find her way back to his hiding spot if she did. At any second she imagined a switchblade-wielding madman would block her path and cut her throat with an elegant swish of his wrist.

The relentless chugging of interlocking gears, the eternal glugging and banging of brass pipes, the rattling of overhead walkways – it all masked the smacking of their shoes against the concrete. In her hurry, Holly almost bashed her forehead against a pressure gauge poking out from behind a pillar. She stared at it in blank surprise. Its arrow was set firmly in the red zone.

"Psst." Fritz's attempt at getting her attention was barely audible amongst the systematic hiss of steam vents and immersion tanks. "Behind here, quick."

She suddenly remembered where she was and hurried behind the cluster of copper-work from which Fritz was waving. He hadn't been kidding when he called it a pipe-wall. All of the pipes from the vats and tanks and cylinders throughout Engineering's various chambers appeared to converge in one central location before shooting up to each respective sector, floor and quarter. There was just enough space to squeeze behind, provided you walked sideways and didn't mind being scalded occasionally. When Holly had asked Fritz about the design back in the hideout, he'd spieled off some convoluted technical explanation about maintenance access and backup diverters and hull integrity. Apparently, you can't go around hanging heavy metal on walls which might be all that's protecting you from a deadly vacuum on the other side.

Holly sucked in her stomach, held her breath as she edged along, and tried not to wince too hard when a film of grease transferred itself onto her cheek from a particularly intrusive valve. Every metal surface felt either too hot or too cold. She tried not to think about how long it would be before she got to have a proper shower and wash all this grime away. With any luck, all memory of this godforsaken space station, too.

"How far?" she whispered.

"Thirty metres or so," he replied. "Curves to the right. Then the elevator is in the next hall over from there."

Holly nodded. Fritz could have said it was a kilometre away for all the choice she had. Hiding behind a dense mesh of plumbing was reassuring in a way, but finding herself trapped behind one if they got caught was too awful to even think about.

Of course, now she couldn't think of anything but.

Fritz gingerly tapped her on the shoulder. She went to say "What?" but her mouth froze open upon seeing the terror on his face.

Slowly, her neck feeling like it was screwed as tight as the thick rivets rubbing against her back, she turned to peer through the pipework.

One of the psychos was standing on the other side, inches away from them. Holly didn't think she recognised him as one of those who'd stalked the halls of Engineering earlier, or as a member of the mob that killed the security team. That there seemed so many of their kind only terrified her more. He was older, with grey, thinning hair spread in a messy combover across a heavily jowled head drenched in perspiration, and with each laboured grunt he further transformed into an obscene grotesquery in the sweltering darkness. He licked his lips excitedly as his eyes, bloodshot and glistening in the dim light, hunted his prey.

A leak from a loose pipe fitting beside Holly's head went *drip, drip, drip*.

She felt like a wounded hiker waiting for a sniffing bear to bite. She didn't dare breathe, let alone continue inching her way to safety. There was nothing to do and nowhere to go. A bead of sweat wriggled down the side of her nose and tried to mountaineer up her nostril. Scrunching her nose only made things worse. Now she needed to sneeze again.

Drip. Drip.

The insane resident lurking no more than a foot from their position rotated as if to study the pipes. Holly was sure he'd seen her through the gaps – their eyes almost seemed to meet for a harrowing second – but then he kept on turning, grunting to himself, grinning and tittering like he'd won a fortune on the slot machines. The man whacked an iron rod against the pipes without warning. Holly and Fritz both jumped; the latter even let out a little bleat of fright. But the man mustn't have heard them, because he laughed – not at their terror, but seemingly at the short, dull *dong* that rang out.

Then, hungrily smacking his lips, he slowly plodded away.

Holly gestured desperately for Fritz to push forward. He seemed too afraid to move. But then, screwing up his face as if in pain, he reluctantly pulled himself further along.

They encountered nothing more dangerous along the rest of the pipe-wall than a filthy, forgotten rag and what looked, to Holly, like a scattering of small, black mouse droppings. She wondered if even space stations as grand as the Saturnalia got pests. All it took was a rodent to stow itself inside one of the supply crates. And if you got a pair, well...

Fritz slipped out of the other side, then lurked skittishly beside the last pressure-relief valve while Holly caught up with him. The giant metal wall to their right possessed a large pair of wheeled shutters that were rolled along tracks to either side and a much smaller door for regular use. With no more tiers of gangways to block their view, the stained, vented ceiling was clearly visible a few dozen metres above her head, and Holly caught a spell of vertigo just looking at it. This hall and the next were already much quieter than the rest of Engineering, though scarcely any cooler.

Sneaking through the smaller door, they discovered high-rise shelving units full of spare parts, jerry-cans and safety equipment. Two forklift trucks were parked nearby, a rusty, busted-up toolkit sitting on one of their leather-padded seats. A pair of fold-out chairs by an overturned wooden crate in the corner suggested that somebody had been in the middle of a card game when the supposed revolution had taken place. From the look of things, neither player had been in possession of a good hand.

Holly blinked heavily in surprise. The maintenance elevator occupied most of the rear wall, surrounded by thick metal pillars sporting cables and gears and brake units, and bordered on all sides by yellow-and-black striped safety barriers. The damn thing was huge. She didn't know why she expected otherwise. If it weren't, there'd be no way to deliver machinery from off-station or get all the engineers downstairs in time for each shift.

"Right. How quickly can we ride it up?"

"We have to bring it down first," Fritz whispered, peering up the shaft. "It's on another sector. Residential, by the look of it."

"Residential? Where the rest of the nutjobs are?" Holly anxiously glanced back the way they came. "Please tell me this elevator's the express kind."

"The opposite." He looked up from the control panel in growing alarm. "This thing's built to lug industrial equipment up and down, not shoot you into the stratosphere. And that's not the worst bit."

"It's not?"

"An elevator like this makes a lot of noise."

Holly exhaled in panicky frustration. The hall outside the elevator was deserted... for now. The waxy fluorescent lamps suspended from the high ceiling flickered on and off. Maybe with all the other machinery running elsewhere, those patrolling the rest of Engineering wouldn't hear it.

"And there's no other way up to the shuttle?"

"Nothing that won't take us on a tour of the whole damn station, no."

"Then I guess we have no choice. We've wasted enough time waiting inside your hideout as it is. Fire it up. If it's too noisy, we can... we can hide behind that."

She pointed behind the overturned crate. Hell, it was pretty big. Maybe they could hide *underneath* it if necessary.

"And they won't look back there, will they?" Fritz asked uneasily.

"Do you have a better idea?" She rapidly tapped her foot against the concrete. "Come on. We're dead anyway if we stay down here much longer."

Fritz shook his head as if telling himself this was a bad move, then slammed his palm against the console's big red button.

The elevator began its thunderous descent. Holly physically jumped at the wallop of sound that signalled its activation – not only mechanical grinding, but a rhythmic bleating from flashing red alarms installed up and down the wall. Goddammit. Features designed to protect lives were now more likely to end them.

She spun around, her heart weakening and her mouth bone dry. Nobody had come running to kill them... yet.

Then, after only a few seconds and maybe a dozen metres of travel, the elevator ground to a halt.

"What's happening?" she asked, racing back to the striped safety barrier. "Did it break?"

"I don't know." Fritz tried punching the button again to no avail. Again and again, nothing. "Maybe it got caught on something? Or someone could have—"

Fritz had been craning his neck for a better look. He gasped and grabbed Holly's arm as he sprinted away from the control panel.

"Get back!"

The elevator came screeching down the shaft much faster than Holly had hoped. Fountains of sparks spat out to either side as steel battled steel. When it emerged through the ceiling of Engineering, its front-left corner hung a good metre or so below the others, and a number of thick wires and cables trailed out behind it like the deadly tentacles of a Portuguese man-o-war. The elevator crashed through the hydraulic pit beneath, cracking the surrounding concrete and spraying out shards of barrier like grenade shrapnel.

"Holy shit," Holly said, picking herself up off the floor. "What the—"

"They cut the brake cables," Fritz gasped, clutching his side. "They knew we were coming. We have to get out of here, now."

"Get out of here? I thought you said there wasn't—"

"*Now!*"

Holly chased Fritz out of the hall housing the maintenance elevator. The psychos from before emerged from behind the pipes and tanks of the next chamber. She swore under her breath and followed Fritz sharply to the right.

"Come back!" the dishevelled woman cackled at them. "We only want to *talk* to you!"

"What'cha wanna go upstairs for?" another man shouted. "Your kind don't *belong* up there!"

Their laughter echoed through the copper labyrinth. Holly assumed they gave chase; she kept her bleary eyes forward in case she brained herself against another burst pipe or pressure gauge. Her arms were covered with goosebumps, the skin on the back of her neck felt like it was stretched thin enough to split, and she desperately wanted to throw up. It was pure fear that kept her legs moving. Her own strength had given up long ago.

The world grew kaleidoscopic. The colours blurred and lone generators split into two then four. She desperately blinked her eyes clear, ignoring the way they stung from her sweat just as she did the leaden ache in her legs. She could hear the monsters running now. The smack of their shoes and bare feet against the hard floor, the screech of their cries, almost drowned out the almighty timpani in her ears.

"This way," she thought she heard Fritz yell from somewhere up ahead.

He knew where to run. She didn't. Every choice to go left or right around the next support strut could result in a dead end or a detour that took her in the total opposite direction. Soon she lost sight of him completely. Her only option was to keep heading forward.

Something flew past her head and smashed into a light fitting. Glass and plastic rained over her. Holly shrieked but kept running. More laughter. Closer, this time. Gaining on her. Seconds from reaching out and snatching her, pulling her roughly to the concrete, cracking her ribs and kicking her head in.

She grew disassociated from herself, numb, as if her body raced on while her mind drifted slowly back, submitting itself to the murderous throng.

A muscular young man in a greasy white t-shirt leapt out from behind a chunky, vertical helium coolant pipe to her left. An enormous grin stretched from both sides of his pale, waxy face. Holly raised her arms in self-defence and shrank back as he pretended to snarl like a rabid dog. Then he took a swing at her. She ducked instinctively and felt his fist pass through her hair. She was lucky he didn't try to grab it. His attempt to trip her up was even less successful. She began sobbing uncontrollably as she hopped over first his leg and then a nest of exposed wires torn from the neighbouring machinery.

"Holly?" The voice was barely audible over the rumble of hungry engines. "Holly, where are you? Hurry, please!"

She felt a sudden lightness take over her. It was Fritz. He hadn't abandoned her. She couldn't be sure where the voice had come from, but she charged forward with renewed fervour.

"Fritz? I don't know where I am!"

"Over here!" Much louder, this time. "I can see you!"

And she could see him. His small, weathered face poked out from inside a metal hatch a dozen metres over. He was manically waving in her direction while his eyes darted everywhere else. She pushed herself all the harder, her lungs burning, knowing that her would-be killers grew closer still.

He reached out and grabbed her as she drew level with the hatch in the wall. She frantically crawled through on her hands and knees, not knowing what lay on the other side, not caring, just thankful that this new darkness wasn't quite as black as the vents.

A hand grabbed her ankle. She looked back and saw the woman in the nightgown lying on the floor behind her. The rest of the frenzied crowd was only seconds from joining in. The first kick Holly delivered to the woman's face didn't so much as dislodge her smile, but the second broke her nose. Free from the woman's grip, Holly tucked her legs inside just as half a dozen more hands shot forward to claw at her.

Fritz slammed the hatch shut behind them. It was designed to swing outwards, and the lunatics immediately began prying it open again. He slammed it shut once more, the tendons on his arms and neck bulging like bridge cables, and Holly stared apathetically at a small spurt of blood near the hinge where somebody's fingers had got caught.

"Lock it!" Fritz screamed at her.

Holly snapped free from her stupor. She bent forward and rotated the two catches at the top and bottom of the hatch. Thick bolts slid into position. Fritz kept a tight grip on the inside handle, straining against it as if he didn't believe the bolts would hold. Perhaps they wouldn't. But then he sagged backwards in exhaustion, even as their would-be killers continued to beat furiously against the other side.

"Up," he wheezed. "We need to go up."

Holly helped pull Fritz to his feet as the thumping on the hatch door intensified. Their new room was cramped – smaller than the storage closet or the hideout, even – and illuminated only by a series of dim, red lights. A towering ladder of galvanised steel, bolted to the back wall and encased by a semi-circular safety cage, rose out of sight.

"What is this?" she asked. "I thought you said there wasn't any way up without the elevator."

"No, I said—" Fritz coughed violently into his sleeve. "I said there was no other way that wouldn't take us on a grand tour of the station. This is a maintenance shaft. There are corridors and tunnels just like this all throughout Saturnalia. Do you really think the lords and ladies upstairs want grease monkeys like me wandering about the station where people might see us?"

"But this'll take us to the Residential District, right?"

Fritz shook his head.

"Just the Workers' District. We'll need to find another way up from there."

They jumped as something heavy was rammed into the hatch behind them. Holly thought she saw the metal panel buckle inwards slightly.

"Get moving," Fritz urged desperately. "Please! That hatch was built to withstand worse than fists and wrenches, but I wouldn't bet my life finding out."

Holly grabbed the first set of rungs and started climbing. She didn't think her legs had any strength left in them, but adrenaline kept them remarkably obedient. Even her arm didn't hurt as much for the moment, though the trickle of blood seeping out from under the dirty rag suggested the wound had reopened itself sometime during the chase. She just concentrated on where she was putting her hands, the feeling of rust beneath her fingers, and tried to keep her eyes up, not down. That's all she could do.

One rung after the other, until the end.

CHAPTER
EIGHT

The hatch at the top of the ladder crashed open. Holly crawled out and collapsed onto the floor beside it, exhausted.

Her chest rising and falling in great swells, she rolled her throbbing head to one side and discovered a discarded ladle lying only a few feet away.

She scrunched up her brow.

Why was there a ladle on the floor?

Fritz clambered out of the hole behind her and slammed the hatch closed again. Scanning the room in a panic, he stepped over Holly, snatched up the ladle and fed it through the handles. Then he found a small serving trolly and rolled it over the top of the hatch for good measure.

"I don't know if that'll hold," he gasped, "but it's better than nothing. Just in case they follow us, you know?"

Holly nodded wearily. The psychopaths in Engineering had still been pounding at the hatch downstairs when she and Fritz had finished their ascent. The more barriers between her and them, the better.

She sat up and cleared her head. Her vision, which had

gone dark around the periphery during the climb, began to return. Her heart rate fell to something below one hundred and thirty beats per minute. Terrified as she was, there was no use in hyperventilating. Raw panic wouldn't keep her alive.

Fritz hurried back from a quick reconnaissance mission.

"Coast looks clear," he said, collapsing against the counter next to her. "We're alone."

"Well, it's no secret we're upstairs." Her chest aching, she rose to her feet. "But do you think any of them know where we are right now?"

Fritz shook his head.

"None of them worked in Engineering. I shouldn't think they'll know specifically where this shaft leads. Up until a few days ago, the whole point was to keep these access tunnels secret from the residents. Out of sight, out of mind."

"Speaking of which. Where *did* this shaft lead, Fritz?"

Once again she found herself in a small, windowless room full to the brim with shelves. Pots and pans and assorted cooking utensils hung from hooks on the walls. Boxes of cleaning products were stacked on every inch of counter space. A small, circular drain was built into the centre of its floor. The air was noticeably cooler than in Engineering – fresher, too, thanks to the absence of choking fumes and stale steam. Her ringing ears were just as grateful as her lungs, though she could have done without the gross sensation of dirty sweat rapidly drying all over her body.

Without opening his eyes, Fritz lethargically waved for her to follow him out through the room's only door.

"I'll show you around. Funny, we haven't had a new arrival since... well, since they brought in Park to replace Fieraru. That was over two years ago."

He paused.

"Though I suppose this place has seen quite a few visitors since the uprising," he added. "Best keep an eye out..."

"Is it an uprising if the upper class kills those below them?" Holly asked nervously. "Wouldn't that technically be a... a downfalling?"

Fritz stopped with the door half open, his face stoney.

"That isn't funny, Holly. My friends are dead."

"Shit. I'm sorry, that was thoughtless of me. I'm just trying not to have a full-on mental breakdown, that's all."

"Hmm."

He finished opening the door, held it for an embarrassed Holly to pass through. No prizes for guessing where they'd ended up now, she supposed. This was definitely the canteen Fritz mentioned earlier. Breakfast, lunch and dinner – every meal the workers ate was served here. One of the most heavily frequented areas on the station, no doubt, third only to wherever they slept and, of course, wherever they worked their shift.

She emerged at the rear of the kitchen, which in turn overlooked a much larger canteen area. A long service counter with room for half a dozen cauldron-size cooking pots and various gastronome pans separated the two. Half of the counter's plexiglass shields had been smashed inwards. Stoves were wrecked, faucets burst, utensils scattered like silver leaves in the fall. Pots were toppled and sticky brown goop poured over the floor. Half of the tables and chairs in the canteen had been overturned. One of the few things left standing was, surprisingly, the cabinet where the dinner trays got stowed.

Everything was either plastic-white or girder-grey. Easily wipeable. The only decorative flourish was a thick red stripe that ran along the top of each wall panel. Maybe it was intended to add a splash of colour and character to the room, but Holly thought it only brought attention to how drab and devoid of charm everything else was. You'd at least expect a motivational poster or two for morale.

"It's not quite as fancy as the welcome lobby," she joked, flashing Fritz a sympathetic smile.

"What did you expect, the Ivy? The founders aren't going to waste money by spending it where they can't see it. And it's not that bad. For what it's worth, the food's actually pretty good. No worse than what we got on the Arks, at any rate."

"You sure about that? I tried one of your protein bars, remember."

"Oh, those are just snacks. They serve ham sandwiches and rice bowls, too. And every now and again we get beef stew, if the meat would go bad otherwise."

"Beef stew? Huh. Maybe I'm in the wrong job."

"The founders might have gone mad, but they weren't stupid. They know a hungry worker isn't a hard worker."

"So it serves their best interests to keep you well-fed," Holly mused. "Somebody crunched the numbers and figured out it saves them money in the long run. Why is that not surprising?"

"You tell me. *You're* the analyst."

Fritz started in alarm. Holly spun around thinking he'd seen someone coming for them, but the canteen was empty.

"Hey," he said, "are you still hungry?"

"Erm, I guess?" Now he mentioned it, her stomach *was* growling. "I've had other things on my mind. Is food really the priority here?"

"I'm famished. Haven't eaten anything real in days. There must be *something* decent left."

Fritz navigated his way around the kitchen's gunky puddles towards the walk-in refrigerator.

"Yeah, something tells me the soup's gone cold," Holly

said. "And I saw the mash potato they were serving. Nothing edible should ever look that colour."

Fritz unstuck the pair of refrigerator doors from their suction-sealed embrace and stared despondently inside.

"Oh, Hank. Not you, too."

Holly tiptoed up behind him and craned to look over his shoulder. A dead body lay face down, sprawled out in the middle of the refrigerator's tiled floor. A small puddle of dark, dry blood spread from a particularly vicious wound on the back of his head. The man was wearing white overalls. Holly wouldn't have described him as a chef exactly, but he certainly looked like he knew his way around a kitchen.

"Did you know him?" Holly asked.

"Everybody did," Fritz sighed. "He was in charge of this place. Three meals a day, seven days a week. Always nodded to each other as I got in line. Goddammit. Why the hell'd they have to kill him, eh? Clearly the poor guy didn't go charging upstairs with everyone else."

He gingerly stepped around the corpse.

"Sorry about this, Hank."

"What, and *this* hasn't put you off your appetite?" Holly asked, surprised.

"Food is fuel." He rummaged through the various boxes and trays lining the shelves. "And right now I feel like I'm running on fumes. I don't know what supplies you've got on that shuttle of yours, but if I don't eat now I might not survive the trip back."

He triumphantly retrieved two transparent, easy-seal bags from a plastic crate.

"Sausage balls. Want one?"

Holly grimaced.

"Yeah, go on, then. It's not like I'm gonna find anything fresher to eat."

Fritz inched around the body and handed one of the bags to Holly. The sausage balls looked gristly. She doubted they'd ever seen any part of a pig. But funnily enough, the longer she held the greasy, ever-so-slightly charred balls of meat, the more delicious they promised to be.

"I guess we'll have to eat them cold," Fritz said, surveilling the ruined kitchen. "We'd probably blow up half of Saturnalia trying to operate this. Still, they'll taste just as good."

He crossed to a table in the middle of the canteen and pulled up a chair.

"You want to eat them here?" Holly said, hurrying after him. "Like, out in the open?"

"Would you prefer to wolf them down inside the fridge?"

Thinking of Hank's body lying there in the cold made her shudder. She didn't much like the idea of being near that hatch in the storage room, either.

"Fair enough. And I suppose this way we'll see people coming. But for God's sake, choose a less conspicuous table."

They sat as close to the kitchen as possible so they had a clear path back to the storage closet – and the hatch that led back down to Engineering – if they needed it. Most of Holly's attention was occupied by the two large sets of double doors to either side of the canteen.

"Which way to the elevator?" she asked, unsealing her bag. "Those doors there, I'm guessing?"

Fritz followed her gaze and nodded. Fortunately for the two of them, somebody had already barricaded the doors from inside the canteen with a broken piece of bench. Or perhaps unfortunately, if the person who'd locked them in was also trying to kill them.

"Uniform repair shop, the bathrooms, and then the maintenance elevator, yes."

Holly risked a bite of her first sausage ball. God, it was glorious. Or maybe she was just delirious. Either way, she could barely keep from smiling as the grease dripped down her fingers.

Definitely delirious, then.

"So we're headed that way, right?"

"Not unless you plan to free-climb up to Residential. The elevator came crashing down, remember?"

She waved half a sausage ball incredulously.

"There aren't stairs in case of an emergency?"

"Holly. If there were stairs, we wouldn't have tried taking the slow and extremely noisy maintenance elevator in the first place."

"Okay. Good point."

"Also, that's where all the crazy people are. Hence, bye-bye elevator." Fritz paused mid-chew. "I mean, the rest of the Workers' District could be just as bad as Engineering. But that's where the access tunnels are, so..."

His own supply depleted, he pointed to Holly's remaining sausage balls.

"They're good, right? So, what's the plan?"

"I thought you knew a way up."

"I do. Well, I *think* I do. It's been a while since they sent me to fix anything that wasn't down in the, you know... the guts."

"Your wife works in the suites, doesn't she?" Holly was baffled. "Didn't she ever show you how she got up there? Didn't you *ask?*"

"We worked the same shifts," Fritz replied, unapologetic. "You think giving each other tours of our commute was the first thing we wanted to do after the whistle went? Besides, I'm not talking about how we're getting upstairs. I'm asking *you* what the plan is once we're there."

Holly popped her penultimate sausage ball into her mouth and used her time chewing to come up with an answer.

"It's simple," she eventually replied. "We get back to the Residential District, we figure out where Rosie Flynn is, and then we all use the shuttle to get the hell off this station. There's no point in nailing down the finer details when everything's subject to change, anyway."

Exasperated, Fritz leaned back in his chair.

"You're still obsessed with finding Mrs. Flynn? *Mein Gott*, you're as mad as everyone else here, you know that? She's dead. Of course she is. Either that or a murderer like everyone else. And who outside of the company really cares what happens to her, anyway? You really want to find someone that bad? Go search for my wife."

Holly clenched her jaw.

"I thought you said *she* was dead."

"Yeah, probably!" He shot forwards again. "So what? If we're going on a wild goose chase, let's at least chase a goose one of us actually gives a shit about."

"It's not as simple as that."

"Like hell it isn't. All you care about is... is... is your damn Flynn Industries pay check! It's like you said back in my hideout – I survived, so maybe Maria did too. You won't get anywhere without me, and I'm not leaving until I know for sure."

"For Christ's sake, Fritz. We don't have time to scour every inch of this station for two different people! We shouldn't even be sitting here eating! If you go off exploring every nook and cranny on Saturnalia, I'll be forced to leave you behind. Sorry."

"We won't be 'going off' anywhere! All I'm asking is we

check in on my quarters to make sure she's not there. It's *on the way*."

Holly snapped her mouth shut and took stock of the situation. Giving the poor man hope had been a mistake, but, like it or not, she still needed Fritz until they got to the shuttle. If he truly wanted to stay behind and search for his wife after that, so be it.

"Shit. Fine. If it's really on the way, then of course we can check in on your digs. But I came here on a mission, Fritz. I can't fail because you decide to suddenly grow a pair and make things personal."

"Fuck you. All we've got is personal. Maria isn't less important than Rosie Flynn just because we're poor."

The two of them sat in silence as the dangling fluorescent lights of the canteen flickered on and off. Fritz eyed the one remaining sausage ball.

"You going to eat that?" he asked impatiently.

"Help yourself," she said, shoving the bag across the table.

CHAPTER
NINE

They were fortunate that the electromagnetic security door connecting the canteen to the larger Workers' District remained operational.

Not a lot else was.

Holly hadn't seen much of Saturnalia besides its atrium and a glimpse of what lay beyond the fateful welcome tunnel – ignoring Engineering, of course – but she was certain those who'd funded the station's construction had it better than this. The corridors were cramped, with tighter walls and lower ceilings to maximise the use of all available space. Suddenly the canteen seemed attractive in comparison – steel and aluminium panelled every wall, the floors were covered in worn diamond treads, and exposed pipes ran along ceilings speckled with gunk and rust. Holly presumed the lights were brighter and more reliable under usual circumstances. Half of the workers' subterranean world was cast into darkness, the other half into disarray.

It was no small mercy that the place was deserted. There wasn't exactly much room to run or hide.

"Normally you can barely squeeze through here, it's so

busy," Fritz whispered. "People are always coming and going – leaving shifts, starting them, everything in between."

"It's crazy how much can change in so little time," Holly replied. Remembering Fritz's wife, she added, "Just because it's quiet doesn't mean everyone's dead, though. Some might still be hiding."

"I hope so." He fidgeted with the sleeve of his uniform and his eyes glistened with fear. "They may not have been my friends, exactly, not *real* friends, but they're still the only people I've known since leaving Earth."

Holly cast her mind back to her office on New Terra, to Aria Nicholson and Brian Edwards and the rest of them with their beady, scrutinising eyes, and couldn't imagine what it would be like to know them and nobody else. To not have friends of her own choosing, to not have the freedom to travel to the next town over and explore, or find a new job, or simply do nothing at all. To be trapped, and be expected to be grateful for it, forever – it was unthinkable.

Not far from the canteen's security door, and past an overturned pallet trolley from down in the warehouse, was a small, unlabelled hole-in-the-wall with a busted-up computer monitor. Most of it had been ransacked, but a few protein bars and tubes of toothpaste still lined the various shelves behind the counter.

"The commissary," Fritz explained, detecting Holly's confusion. "Snacks, toiletries, erm, women's needs. A few specialty items from time to time."

"You earn a salary? I thought you were stuck here while you paid off your Ark tickets."

"Of course we get paid," Fritz laughed as they continued onwards. "We're not slaves, even if we do owe Flynn Industries our lives. Most of our wages go towards bed and board, that's all. And what's left could never cover the cost of a private shuttle off-station, no matter how long we saved up for. But we can spend it however we see fit, you know, provided what we want's on board."

"Justify it to yourself however you like," Holly said uneasily, "but if you're stuck working on Saturnalia forever, that sure sounds like slavery to me."

"Well, you don't live here, so you don't know. What's the old saying? Better to die free than live as slaves, right? Well, that's bullshit. Pride's the worst sin of all, and if you're dead, you're dead. I'd much rather be stuck here with my wife than both of us blister to death on our abandoned homeworld."

"Yeah, you've got me there. I guess you could say we're the lucky ones, if you think about it."

Fritz said nothing.

They passed a set of bathrooms. With so much adrenaline and cortisol coursing through her body, Holly honestly wasn't sure if she needed to go or not. She was too scared to venture inside any of their darkened cubicles by herself, anyway, and she sure as hell wasn't inviting Fritz in with her.

"How far to the workers' quarters?" she asked. "No offence, but this place really gives me the fucking creeps."

"They're pretty close, though it's a bit of a walk until we get to where Maria and I stay. It's not much of a detour," he added quickly, in case Holly protested again. "They like to keep the staff as near to the showers and canteen and elevator as possible. Cuts down on tardiness."

The commissary wasn't the only store they came across, though each was just as un-signposted and nondescript. Sometimes tucked down narrow perpendicular corridors, she wouldn't have even known they were there had Fritz not pointed them out. Nothing more than market stalls dug out of the dirty metalwork. All as gutted and butchered as the last.

Holly sniffed. Iron, or maybe copper. Yes, the whole station was full of the stuff, but the stench was even more prominent than usual – a tanginess that stung the nostrils.

She glanced casually to her right, took a sharp breath, and shrank back against the opposite wall.

More graffiti written in human blood.

And it was still wet.

"*We were blind*," she read, frantically glancing each way down the corridor for the culprit. "What the hell is that even supposed to mean?"

"I'm not sure it means anything," Fritz replied, hunching his shoulders. "You saw how unhinged everyone's got. They probably—"

A metallic *thud* as something dropped down around the next corner. A pile of trash bags, no doubt abandoned on their way to a compactor chute, slipped and spilled their innards across the corridor floor.

"What the hell was that?" Fritz hissed.

"What do you think?" Holly replied, urgently scanning the cramped hallway for something she could use as a weapon.

A slow, sharp tapping sound. They instinctively drew closer to one another, resigned to the knowledge that there was nowhere safe to run...

The culprit trotted out and meowed.

"Holy shit," Holly gasped. "It's just a damn cat."

"My God," Fritz whispered. "It must have escaped from the suites. I didn't even know they were allowed pets on the station. Is it a real one, do you think? I haven't seen a cat since, well, you know."

"It's damn realistic if it isn't. Here, kitty."

The ginger tabby took one look at her, hissed, and then scampered off into the darkness again.

"Hey, don't be sad," Fritz said. "Once you rescue Mrs. Flynn, maybe you can ask her to buy you one."

"Very funny. Just get us to the sleeping quarters before something really does try to kill us."

They walked slower and less confidently going forward, afraid to let so much as a hollow knock ring out. The engineer was right, though – the residential area of the Workers' District wasn't far. Nor was it any more desirable than the rest of the sector. It was signposted, however. Or rather, the clusters of quarters were. *A1-20* on the left, *B1-20* on the right, and so on down a wide, central aisle flanked by industrial support arches.

A woman was slumped against the wall next to the first set of B quarters. She had a fancy housekeeping uniform on, the sort one would expect those working in high-end hotels to wear. Fritz hurried over and checked her pulse, but it was obvious the woman was long dead. The bloody metal bottle used to club her lay only a few feet away.

"Do you recognise her?" Holly asked quietly.

"No." He stood up and stuffed his hands into the pockets of his overalls. "Maybe she worked with Maria, but I never met her."

"Where did you and your wife stay?" She wanted to say *live,* but arguably the whole station was his home, and *sleep* felt patronising somehow.

"B-89."

Increasing his pace and paying the signs no mind, Fritz made a beeline for the cluster in question. Holly struggled to keep up, not because she was exhausted – though she was – but out of fear that their enthusiasm would attract killers of a slightly less feline variety. Especially as it soon became apparent than the maid wasn't the only victim – two men, one rich toff from up top and another engineer who wasn't about to be identified by his dental records any time soon, joined her in the central aisle alone.

If Maria was down here somewhere, Holly didn't hold out much hope they'd find her breathing. Rosie Flynn, on the other hand, had far greater odds of survival. When it came to security, the rich weren't stupid. They always had contingencies in place. Panic rooms and sector lockdowns, that sort of thing.

Or so she had to hope, lest her whole trip be for nothing.

B81-99. The last set of quarters on the right-hand side. Fritz ducked into it at a sprint. Holly let him run ahead. She knew where to find him. And if his careless desperation brought a wave of psychos crashing down on them... well, at least she'd have a few extra seconds to get away.

"Maria?" She winced as Fritz's voice filled the halls as perilously as a deadly nerve toxin. "Are you there, Maria? It's me! It's Fritz!"

The man was a damn idiot, but she couldn't blame him. It doesn't matter how pessimistic somebody is – the second you light even the tiniest flicker of hope in their heart, they secretly become the world's biggest optimist. She just hoped whatever the poor man discovered didn't render him too distraught to show her the way out of this madhouse.

Each lodging had its own lockable door, most of which were busted open. For some reason Holly had imagined the sort of bunks common to hostels and the Ark ships – coffin-sized cubicles with nothing but a pull-across curtain for privacy. The workers' quarters on Saturnalia were far from luxurious, and they were certainly smaller than even the modest apartment Holly had back on New Terra, but they offered more dignity than she'd come to expect from this place.

The reason, she suspected, was obvious. *A sane worker is a happy worker*, or something along those lines. They were expected to spend practically their whole lives within these four walls – when they weren't hard at work, of course. If she'd been brought in to analyse worker wellbeing in a bid to reduce sick days (and therefore the company's overhead), she would have advised the same thing.

Still, there were prison cells with more real estate.

Fifteen square metres – three by five. Not a huge degree of headroom, but even the lankiest employee could be confident they wouldn't brain themselves against the ceiling, which boasted both an air vent *and* an encaged lightbulb. The walls were plasterboard painted a bright, sea-salt grey. A no-nonsense double bed occupied half of the room, complete with a pair of pillows and duvet, all white. A small table and two plastic chairs – sometimes with cushions – in one corner, a wardrobe/chest of drawers combo in the other. Some rooms were more cosy and custom-decorated than others, with rugs and drapes and various bric-a-brac and curios brought from Earth. There was no kitchenette, nor a toilet or shower, but the workers' canteen was always open due to the overlap in day and night shifts, and the communal bathrooms were only a short walk down the hall.

Some rooms were exactly as their tenants left them, the beds made and linen folded. Others had been vandalised beyond repair. She stumbled across two more corpses before her inspection was over, and the wall separating B83 from B85 had been knocked straight through.

"Maria?"

Still no response from his wife, and a lot of the conviction was sapped from Fritz's voice. Holly guessed his search wasn't going well. Then again, perhaps they should both be glad it hadn't gone badly, either.

"She isn't here," Fritz said softly as her shadow fell across the doorway of B89. The room was a mess, though whether this was down to Fritz or passing madmen was unclear. He still appeared to be searching for something – surely not his wife, unless she was the size of a thimble.

Their 'home' was fairly nondescript in that it hardly stood out from the rest of the lodgings, but personal touches included a tower of small, felt baskets and a framed picture of the couple – happier, their arms around one another, at some kind of party or private function back on Earth – sitting on the small table. The glass was cracked but the photograph underneath was undamaged. Holly squeezed past Fritz and picked it up for a closer look.

"Maria's beautiful," she said, raising both eyebrows. "You've been punching above your weight, friend."

"Her necklace," Fritz replied, distractedly pulling open the drawers of their wardrobe. "It's gone. I can't find it anywhere."

"Might she be wearing it?" Holly suggested.

"I wouldn't think so. She never took it with her when she went on a shift. Too valuable. Not priceless in a money sense, you know, just its sentimental value. It was an heirloom given to her by her mother before she died, and her mother before that. We didn't bring much else with us…"

He stood up straight, his search exhausted.

"No, she didn't have it on her when she set off for work the morning everything went wrong. I'm sure of it. So either one of the mad bastards broke in and stole it, or… or Maria found a way down here before going off to hide somewhere else. Yes, that must be it."

Holly hadn't the energy to point out the flaw in his hopeful logic, let alone to carry her through the inevitable argument with him if she did. Normally she'd say that denial was stupid, but if it kept him going long enough to get inside the shuttle, it might just save his life.

"Something's got me thinking," she said, changing the topic. "I understand why the workers might revolt against the rich, given you're all stuck down here doing hard labour while they get to live off the spoils upstairs like kings and queens. But a pretty big share of the violence seems to be targeted towards your lot, Fritz. And it doesn't look like self-defence to me. It *looks* like some of them deliberately came down here intending to wipe everybody out. But what the hell would possess them to do that? Excuse me for being insensitive, but their lavish lifestyle isn't going to last all that long without servants to do everything for them."

"Are you suggesting that us workers did something to set them off?"

"No! Of course not, that would be absurd. I'm just saying that nothing about this situation makes sense, that's all."

"Make sense? Why on earth would it make sense?" Fritz collapsed onto his bed with his head in his hands. "All I know is what other people were shouting. I've been trying to tell you this from the start."

Something groaned deep in the station. Just the metal frames shifting as temperatures climbed and fell, most likely – the sort of sound that was perhaps reassuring to those who lived amongst the stars. But Holly didn't like its ominous clanking all the same. Saturnalia sounded hungry.

"Yes, well, we'd better keep moving. Your wife's not here, but somebody else might be. Where's this maintenance tunnel to Residential you talked about?"

Fritz shut his eyes and balled his hands into fists, scrunching up his bedcovers in the process, then nodded irritably.

"You're right. It isn't safe here. The housekeeper tunnels

that lead up to the suites – the ones Maria used to get to work – are probably located in the laundry room. But I know for sure there's one a little further past that, one that'll take us closer to the atrium."

"How close?"

"As close as we're gonna get from down here," Fritz replied with a shrug. "Certainly now the maintenance elevator's *kaputt*. Take it or leave it."

"Obviously I'm going to take it," Holly said, sighing exasperatedly. "I mean, shit. Forgive me for wanting to avoid as many of those psychos as possible."

"Whatever." Fritz rose from the bed. "I said I'd get you to your shuttle, and I will. But if this is gonna work, *you'll* need to follow *me*. Got it?"

Holly raised her hands.

"You're the boss. It's not like I'm finding my way off this station without you."

"Exactly," he said, striding out of B89. "Now, let's go pay a visit to the priest."

CHAPTER
TEN

Holly caught up with Fritz as they passed through the automatic security door at the other end of the workers' quarters.

"I'm sorry," she whispered. "Did you say a *priest?*"

"Yes, Father O'Brien." Fritz seemed to not find this unusual. "He leads the parish here on Saturnalia."

Holly tried to process this as they strolled down the dark and chilly corridor beyond. Sparks spilled noisily from large, overloaded ventilation fans to either side of them.

"Sorry, the *parish?*"

"He has quite the flock." Fritz frowned. "Not just Christians, if that's what you're worried about. Father O'Brien has always been very welcoming of those from other faiths as well."

"Oh, I'm not questioning the priest's religious tolerance. I'm questioning why you have a priest on the space station at all."

They rounded the next corner.

"Well, I suppose—Oh, shit. Well, that's not good."

The entire hallway had collapsed in on itself. Water

gushed from burst pipes, severed cables flapped about in the puddles, and half of the ceiling's supports had pulled free from their rivets. Even if they could squeeze themselves through the gaps in the debris, the electrified waterfalls would fry them.

"Is this somebody on board's doing," Holly whispered, fearfully glancing back the way they came, "or is Saturnalia already falling apart?"

"The core systems should have safeguards in place to prevent accidents like this even if there aren't any workers around to keep an eye on things. Saturnalia's too big an investment to leave in the hands of a few mechanics. But somebody could have disabled those safeguards, if they knew how. Like what Mikhailov intended to do, before..."

Fritz shuddered as he remembered the worker pinned to the wall back in Engineering.

"Or somebody could have gone crazy and torn it all apart, I suppose," he conceded.

"I take it there's another way around?"

"Of course. It wouldn't be much good if people got stuck in one part of the station, especially if that included the person sent to fix the problem. Hence the maintenance tunnels. But we can just head through Laundry. This way."

He led her on a short detour down a narrow corridor to their right. It wasn't a tight squeeze because the steel walls were too close together, but because most of the corridor's length was occupied by sacks of dirty clothes and bedsheets. Housekeeping wasn't responsible for cleaning just the residents' dirty garments, Holly guessed, but the laundry of the workers, too.

Another security door parted rather begrudgingly and Holly found herself faced with a dozen huge, industrial washers and driers on one side, numerous folding tables and sinks in the room's centre, and enormous cupboards of fresh towels and sheets on the wall opposite. The lighting was particularly bright and artificial here, likely to ensure that no stain ever went unscrubbed, and everything smelled strongly of detergent. It sure made a pleasant change to oil and blood. Somewhere, a tap was dripping.

"Didn't you say there was an access tunnel from somewhere inside Laundry?" she asked.

"That's my understanding, yes."

"And you never thought to come here before?"

"I did, once. Maria needed to work especially late one evening, and since my shift was already over I thought I'd come down and surprise her. Embarrassing, she said it was. But no, I can't say I felt much compulsion to watch sheets get washed."

"Yeah, fair enough. It's not like I've gone out of my way to inspect each and every room inside the Flynn office building, either."

A porthole the size of a dinner plate caught Holly's eye. A billion stars twinkled back at her from the other side.

"Holy shit," she gasped, rushing over to it. "Look at that view."

"Ah, yes." Fritz barely gave it a second glance. "The best look at the great outdoors you'll find down here, that's for sure. I don't know why the architect put a window in here, but there it is. Not that Maria and the girls appreciated having it all that much. They said it reminded them how close they were to a suffocating void."

"Are you sure they weren't talking about the toffs upstairs?" Holly replied, unable to pry herself from the glass.

"Heh." He laughed sadly. "Maybe."

"I didn't realise until now, but this is the first time I've looked at the stars from, you know, out in space. Since the

Ark, that is. The shuttle doesn't have any windows, and until now... well. God, I'd forgotten how beautiful they look."

"I'll take your word for it. Shouldn't we be getting upstairs? I thought you were in a hurry."

Holly pursed her lips and considered her options. Tread carefully, girl.

"The service tunnel your wife used went from Laundry up to the suites, right? Do you know if Lewis and Rosie Flynn lived in the suites with everyone else?"

"Everyone who was a shareholder in Saturnalia had apartments there," Fritz replied. "Didn't Mrs. Flynn tell you when she asked you to come get her?"

Holly bit her lip. She'd tie herself into knots if she wasn't careful. She turned away from the porthole.

"No, she didn't. But if we can take a path straight up there, it might make more sense to rescue Mrs. Flynn *before* heading to the shuttle. You know, just in case we draw any attention to ourselves along the way."

And to make sure you don't bail on me before I get what I came here for, she added to herself.

"Well, the service tunnels do make it easier to move around undetected, but the suites are probably crawling with crazies after everything that happened. Besides, I can't imagine where the hatch might be." Fritz laughed nervously. "Maybe it's hidden under one of the washing machines. I think I saw something like that in an old television show once."

"Hey, didn't you say your wife was up there when the attack started?" Holly returned her gaze to the stars. "Maybe she..."

Holly turned as cold as the vacuum outside.

"Erm, Fritz?" She frantically waved him over. "What in the holy hell is *that?*"

A large white orb, similar in size and shape to a deep sea bathysphere submersible, slowly grew larger outside the window. Across its front was a long, narrow, black slit, and arms like lobster claws extended from either side of it. The object appeared to navigate towards them using a complicated array of air jets.

"Is it another shuttle?" she asked hopefully. "A back-up team?"

"No, that's the EVA pod. They use it for repairing the station's exterior hull. Replacing panels, realigning dishes – that sort of thing. I'm not on that team, of course," he added. "I did run some tests on their docking procedure once, though."

"Okay. Follow up question. Why are they using it to fix the outside of the station when everything *inside* is in a far worse state of disrepair?"

"Maybe they got stuck out there when the revolt happened?" Fritz suggested. "I'll see if I can get their attention."

"For three days? Without food or water?" Holly puffed out her cheeks. "I'm impressed they're still alive. It's not surprising they want to come and wave for help."

Fritz's eyes grew wide.

"Yeah, actually, I don't think they have 'help' on their mind..."

He pulled away from the porthole sharply and backed into one of the laundry room's sinks. Confused, Holly pressed her face against the glass once more.

"Oh. Shit."

One of the pod's lobster claws had extended some kind of drill. Holly leaped backwards as its whirring tip struck the other side of the window. A high-pitched whine filled Laundry.

"If they crack that glass, this whole room will depressurise." Fritz sprinted for the security door on the opposite side of the room. "All of the oxygen will be sucked out. We really don't want to be in here when that happens."

"You think?" Holly chased after him. "Of *course* the corridor outside was blocked. They lured us into a fucking trap."

"This is not a good way to go," he manically muttered to himself. "This is *not* a good way to go..."

The security door was only half a dozen metres away. She hopped over a hillock of mouldy bath towels and shower rugs. Nothing seemed to exist outside of the eternal screeching of high carbon steel against fused silica. The window had to be a few feet thick, at least. It would have been insane to install anything less than that, even in the Workers' District. Surely they had—

The glass cracked.

It didn't shatter, nor had the drill itself pierced all the way through. But enough of a fracture had formed that air got sucked out at an alarming rate. The high-pitched screech was instantaneously replaced with a deafening, buffeting whistle.

A thick shield slammed down over the security door in front of them just as they got within reach of its motion sensor. Holly spun around; a similar shutter blocked the door leading back into the corridor, too.

"Come on!" she screamed, pounding the impenetrable wall with her fists. "Please tell me you can fix this, Fritz."

"I think I can override the lockdown," he said, prying at a panel beside the door. "Fuck, I don't have my tools!"

"Figure something out!"

Holly tried to see if the pod was still drilling at the window, but it hurt to look back towards the crack in the glass, as if it were trying to suck the eyeballs out of her skull. She could still breathe fine, though it felt a little like trying to do so whilst sticking her head out of a fast-moving vehicle. She had to imagine the drill was still going. If the person piloting the EVA pod was even half as insane as those wandering about inside Saturnalia, they weren't likely to leave this job half done.

Fritz darted about in search of something he could use in place of a screwdriver. He found a crooked coat hanger on one of the tables, wedged it between the edges, and pushed. The panel clattered to the floor and then skidded across it towards the growing fissure. A rapid beeping noise spat out from somewhere inside the tangled wires beneath.

"Ah, *halt deinen Mund...*"

Holly was too overwhelmed to move. Breathing became more difficult. Her fingernails dug deeper and deeper into the cotton laundry sacks behind her. Her impending death cycled through her mind over and over again. Her heart was pumping in her mouth. Would it hurt? Of course it would hurt. But would her organs violently rupture from the lack of pressure, or would she slowly suffocate and freeze to death, left to float like a boggle-eyed popsicle inside this derelict space station forever?

Fritz glanced over his shoulder, winced as the wind whipped at his face, waved erratically to get Holly's attention.

"Find something to plug that hole," he screamed at the top of his lungs. "Anything! Just keep the air in here!"

Plug the hole? Like hell was she going anywhere *near* the hole! Her innards would get sucked out like milkshake through a straw. She edged along the back wall, squinting so hard her eyes were almost shut, holding onto the shelves with one hand and shielding her face with the other. She accidentally dislodged a felt-lined box and a bunch of clean aprons spilled out onto the damp floor.

That gave her an idea.

She pulled herself along the shelves like she was scaling the sheer wall of a mountain, afraid to let go for too long in case she went skidding backwards towards the breach. What remained of the oxygen in the room tore at her shirt, billowing it out behind her like a grease-streaked flag. It felt as if the dark cosmos itself was bleeding in and clawing at her.

Napkins and fancy serviettes. Holly threw that box aside. Dish rags from the workers' canteen. No, they were too thin, too small. If the crack in the glass grew – and it would – they'd slip right through. She needed something that was flexible, but also had a little weight behind it.

Bath towels. Thick, fluffy and expensive bath towels. She found a tidy stack of them on the far end of the shelving unit. You could wrap a damn cow inside one of them, they were so big. She grabbed one off the top and flung it in the direction of the porthole.

It fell short, flapped erratically across the floor like a dying fish, and then pinned itself between the wall and a washing machine.

No good. She needed to get closer.

Snatching up the rest of the towels, Holly relinquished her grip on the shelves and inched her way towards the sinks and folding tables in the centre of the room. She couldn't even glance at the porthole anymore. She felt lightheaded and every fibre of muscle in her body ached. Yet she plucked a second towel from the pile and lobbed it towards the crack.

Success! Well, half a success, perhaps. The towel, caught in the suction, had flattened itself against the window. It was too thick to get pulled through the hole, but not so heavy that it couldn't be held in place by the force of the vacuum.

She tried again. The third projectile missed, content to writhe ineffectively around the steel skirting board connecting the wall and floor. With the fourth Holly aimed a little higher, and to her ecstatic relief it folded across the top half of the crack. The hole wasn't completely sealed – if anything, the whistling grew even higher in pitch – and the further the pod drilled through the window the less chance those towels had of staying in place... but she was happy to take the win.

"I did it!" she went to shout. But the words came out in a scratchy rasp. Her throat burned and her lungs hitched. She raised her hand to her neck and stumbled back towards the exit.

Of course. There wasn't enough air left in Laundry. The ventilation shafts must have sealed themselves off the second those shutters went down. Saturnalia couldn't risk losing its entire artificial atmosphere to a single breached sector. No air was getting pumped in to replace that which had been lost.

Even if the porthole held, even if they lost no more oxygen through the crack... they'd suffocate to death in there.

Fritz was coughing and spluttering as he dutifully switched one wire for another. His eyes were streaming, his legs buckling out from under him. The incessant bleeping noise had stopped, but the lockdown was just as in effect as ever.

"One... last... connector," he wheezed.

Something clicked. Tricked into thinking the breach was over, the metal shutter snapped back up into its alcove above the security door. But instead of an open doorway, Holly was met with a blast of air that hit as hard as a truck.

She smacked her hip against the side of a sink as she lost her balance and fell to one knee. Now the wind was *screaming*, too fast and sharp to peer through – almost too powerful a gust to fight against. She pulled herself along the tables, unable to even stand properly, until her palm smacked impotently against the sharp corner, then empty air.

A hand reached out and grasped her own.

She let herself be pulled over to him, pushing against the torrent until she, too, could grab hold of the handles surrounding the laundry room's security door. Fritz tried to shout something, but even a few inches from his face, she couldn't hear him. He pointed desperately to the corridor outside.

Behind them, the glass of the porthole continued to crack.

Together they pulled themselves along handles set into the tiled walls. Fritz crossed first, then reached back to grab Holly's arm as she went to follow. She didn't care. Survival came a long way before personal boundaries. He fought to pass through the open security door, then clung to the industrial handle by the bypass panel on the other side.

"I can't," Holly shouted to him, shaking her head. The tide of air was too powerful, her body too weak to follow. She could feel her sweaty palms losing their grip.

Fritz clambered back, grabbed her by the forearm, and strained to pull her to safety. She reached past him, slipped backwards as her shoes lost grip, then used the last of her energy to throw herself towards the closest pipe...

...just as the porthole shattered outwards and the thick shield door came thundering back down behind them.

They collapsed onto the cold floor of the corridor beyond, their chests undulating like accordions. Save for their wheezing, the space station was totally silent. It was a good couple of minutes before either of them could summon the strength to speak.

"Hey," Holly gasped. "Look on the bright side. I don't think anyone's following us."

"Oh, yeah. *Wunderbar*." Fritz picked himself up and adjusted his twisted overalls. "And to think I was worried there was no turning back."

CHAPTER
ELEVEN

H iding was natural but unnecessary. Nobody came looking for them after the depressurisation of Laundry. With the main corridor blocked and the laundry room an inaccessible vacuum, following in Holly and Fritz's footsteps was impossible, and it seemed as if those responsible had abandoned the way ahead.

Holly hoped the cat they saw was all right.

The rest of their journey took longer than it should have due to their regular breaks spent coughing and retching. Holly spotted a few specks of blood on her fist after a particularly violent bout of chest-hitching, and hoped their near-death experience hadn't inflicted any lasting damage. Of course, with her life expectancy having taken a nosedive ever since setting foot on Saturnalia, maybe it wasn't anything she needed to worry about.

She spat out a globule of coppery phlegm, wiped her nose with the back of her hand, and staggered onwards.

"Is there a prize for guessing which door is the church's?" she asked, leaning against the corner of the corridor.

Unlike the commissaries, which lacked signage and

seemed cobbled together using whatever spare space the occupants could find, the entrance to the church appeared to have been part of Saturnalia's design from the start. The door was of an old, push-pull design rather than the automatic, motion-sensor models found elsewhere around the station, and was adorned with a curved, overhanging portico fitted with bright, inset lightbulbs. A large metal cross, brass against the wall's steel backdrop, hung directly above.

"We'll be safer inside," Fritz said, pushing open the door. "God, I hope Father O'Brien is okay…"

Holly pushed herself off the wall and tottered after him. She wasn't entirely convinced that inside the church would be any less dangerous than outside, but the only option left was to push forwards. As for the priest's odds of survival… well, in this place? She wouldn't put money on a pacifist.

The door creaked as she stumbled through.

"Christ Almighty. Sorry," she quickly added, remembering where she was. "I take it this place has seen better days."

"Those monsters," Fritz said. He stood in the middle of the hall, gobsmacked. "Is there really nothing they won't destroy?"

The church, even in its present state, was considerably more stylish than the rest of the Workers' District. Half of the wooden pews were splintered in the middle or turned over, but in better times there would have been room for two hundred and fifty, maybe three hundred members of a congregation to sit at a time. A pulpit from which Father O'Brien presumably delivered his sermons stood at the front of a small stage towards the back. Two more doors flanked the rear wall to either side of it. Above the stage was another cross, this one carved from rich oak, measuring approximately eighteen feet by ten feet, and showcasing a crucified

Jesus. The high walls to either side of the central nave were covered in ripped ruby curtains spliced with fake (though undeniably beautiful) stained glass windows depicting various scenes from the Old Testament. A couple of these had been shattered to reveal bright spotlights hidden in the alcoves behind.

No wonder it was so popular. It was the only room in the lower sectors that didn't give the impression you were stuck inside a tin can.

Holly sagged onto one of the few benches still intact. She was starting to feel better already, but what she really needed was a moment of freakin' rest.

"They really went all out on recreating the Old World church experience, didn't they? Looks like they cut down actual trees from New Terra." She gasped with sudden realisation. "Shit. Do you think they brought this wood from *Earth?*"

"I know they did," Fritz sighed with a tired smile. "That's what made this place so special. It really felt like home."

Holly couldn't help herself. She reached across to the end of her pew where it had been split by some kind of blunt object and quickly snapped off a splinter. It was pocketed before Fritz could notice.

"I still think it's insane that a place like this exists on Saturnalia, by the way. Isn't it a bit... you know... archaic?"

"Plenty of people still believe in a higher power," Fritz replied, his posture stiffening. "I know it's not as popular a position to take as it once was, what with everything that's happened, but religion hasn't gone extinct. I think people find it comforting."

"Sure, I get that. I mean, who *doesn't* feel more lost than ever these days?" Holly filled her lungs, exhaled deeply. "I'm not saying people shouldn't believe in something, by any means. But a whole church? On a space station like this? Come on, man."

Fritz scowled.

"I'm not sure I follow."

"Yes, you do. The church has always been used to keep the poorest people in society in line. What do you think the promise of heaven is all about? 'Yeah, your life sucks right now, but don't do anything about it while you're still shuffling along the mortal coil. You'll be rewarded for your hard work in the next life, promise.'"

"Are you suggesting the company planted Father O'Brien in the Workers' District to keep us from rocking the boat?"

"Maybe." Holly shrugged. "Or perhaps it's just a massive coincidence that so many of you seem to have adopted religion since your arrival. But if you were going to plant a priest somewhere, it would be here, right? Hundreds of workers stuck inside a hot, grimy basement, unable to quit or leave or improve their lot in life, while the richest men and women in the galaxy parade about like peacocks right above their heads. It's practically begging for a revolution. If you were Flynn Industries, wouldn't you take steps to stop it from happening?"

"Pfft. I don't know." Fritz raised his arms in gesture to the scene around them, then let them slap back down against his sides. "Fat lot of good it did them."

He plucked one of the many ancient Bibles off the floor. Most of its thin pages were shredded.

"Even if you don't believe..." He shook his head and dropped the Bible back to the ground. "I mean, it's a waste of good paper. You don't really see many books these days."

"Not outside of a data pad, no." The worst of her aches having subsided somewhat, Holly rose from her bench.

"Still, it's all a bit weird. It sure seems like Saturnalia got super non-religious all of a sudden."

"What do you mean?"

She pointed to the writing scrawled across the floor beneath Fritz's feet. He jumped aside in surprise.

"*Lies*," he read numbly.

The graffiti wasn't alone. Similar ramblings were smeared across the stage, ornate windows and even the rear of the main door using blood, supplies stolen from the canteen, and Holly didn't even want to hazard a guess as to what else.

"*Blasphemy*," she read aloud. "*Heresy*. Good grief. Somebody sure wasn't happy with your priest, Fritz. Or what he stood for."

"I suppose I shouldn't feel too sad," he replied, still a little stunned. "The church is only going to be destroyed alongside the rest of the station when Saturnalia falls apart, anyway. And it's not like there's anyone left to attend service."

"Do you reckon the residents did this?" Holly crossed to the other side and righted a toppled candelabra. The wax smelled of vanilla. "Maybe Father O'Brien developed a guilty conscience and told the workers what was really going on."

"Maybe he did tell them, and this is what the workers did in retaliation," Fritz said despondently. "I don't know, Holly. I saw some terrible things back on Earth, but... well, that was different. I didn't realise people were actually capable of things like this."

"We crossed the stars and left most of our species behind to die," Holly said, picking out the wax from underneath her fingernail. "After that, I'm ready to believe we're capable of anything."

Fritz jerked his head up as if possessed, then hurried

over to the door to the right of the pulpit. A quick inspection of the small room beyond later, he emerged shaking his head.

"He's not here. Father O'Brien, I mean. I thought maybe... that he..."

"Perhaps, sometimes, it's better not to find a body." Holly joined him beside the pulpit. "If he had any sense, he would have taken that secret passage of his at the first sign of trouble."

She paused mid-breath.

"Hold on. Father O'Brien wasn't a founder, was he?"

"Erm, not that I'm aware of, no."

"Then why the hell would the architects install a maintenance shaft in the back of the man's church in the first place? Didn't he live down here with the rest of you?"

"He had his own quarters, there," he replied, nodding back at the door through which he briefly entered. "But he had to visit the upper districts quite often. Some of the residents needed spiritual guidance, too."

"Uh huh." Holly raised an incredulous eyebrow. "Of course he did. Definitely not a stooge at all."

"Stop it." Fritz barged past her. "You know what? I don't care if they put Father O'Brien here to keep us in line. You're right, he probably was a plant, or a stooge, or whatever. But I think he still believed in everything he told us. And I believe it, too."

"Hey, I'm sorry." Holly raised her hands in an admission of guilt. "I wasn't trying to offend you or mock your belief. I was just questioning the company's motives, that's all. Forget about the lunatics who've moved in. The more I see of this place, the more I think there was something sick about Saturnalia from the start."

"Yeah." Fritz held open the door to the priest's private exit. "About that, you might be right."

The shaft behind the church was slightly more spacious than the one connecting Engineering to the workers' canteen. About as poorly lit, though. Holly had expected stairs, something akin to a New York fire escape or even, if the founders truly were in league with the priest, the bland stairwell of an office building. You couldn't expect a man of the cloth to climb a hundred rungs of a ladder every other evening, after all. But Father O'Brien had his own private elevator. It was a rickety old thing, the kind you might expect to have found in the lobby of a hotel during the Great Depression, but it sure beat scaling a whole sector on foot.

"How'd you even know this was here?" she whispered, her voice drifting up the empty shaft.

"I didn't. Solomon Davis told me about it after he had to head over and swap out some wires once. But Father O'Brien was always honest about it, or he certainly was after that. I mean, if the rest of us all have service tunnels to get from A to B, why shouldn't he?"

"Sure, fair enough. And this thing still works, does it?"

"Unless the residents upstairs have cut the brakes to this elevator, too," Fritz replied with a painfully forced smile.

"Only one way to find out," she said, stepping into the elevator.

The cabin was tight, with enough room for the both of them provided they stood shoulder to shoulder. Holly suddenly wondered if the elevator could actually support their combined weight. Presumably it was accustomed to ferrying just the one man. She supposed they could ride it upstairs one at a time, but she didn't fancy being left down-stairs any more than Fritz probably did.

Too late now, anyway. With them both inside, Fritz pulled the rattly cage door across the front of the elevator. There was only a single button on the panel set beside it. He turned to Holly with an anxious, withered expression on his face.

"Ready?" he asked, clearly wishing she'd say no. She wondered when he'd last been up to the 'surface' sectors.

"Can't hide down here forever," she replied, reaching across and giving the button a push.

The entire cabin shook with a terminal *clunk*. Nothing happened. The damn thing was busted like everything else. But then, just as Holly was getting ready to jab at the button like a hyperactive woodpecker, the gears and pulleys kicked into lethargic action.

Croaking and clanging, and trembling even worse than Holly's hands, the priest's elevator trundled its way up into the Residential District.

CHAPTER
TWELVE

The elevator arrived without fanfare. It simply... stopped. No friendly chime to signal the end of its journey, no sudden reveal of either paradise or a salivating crowd of madmen. Dusty metal walls surrounded the cabin. Holly might have believed they were trapped halfway up the maintenance shaft had it not been for the cobwebbed ceiling lurking so close overhead.

Fritz, after a couple of hesitant starts, pulled the safety gate across. He did so as slowly as he could, yet it still rattled. Holly winced. This was the worst time to attract attention to themselves. Nowhere to run or hide. Even if they managed to get the elevator running again before anyone reached them, they were trapped.

"Erm, Fritz? Don't you think we're missing something?"

The wall in front of them was as bland and dusty as everything else in the shaft. She at least expected an old, wooden door like the one down in the church, if not something sensor-activated. But there was nothing. Well, nothing except for the small but conspicuous gap past the lip of the cabin and the long, dark drop waiting beneath.

"Now, what did Solomon say?" Fritz muttered to himself. "I think... Ah, yes..."

He reached across the gap – Holly felt compelled to grab the back of his overalls, just as he'd grabbed onto her in the laundry room – and patted the left side of the wall in front of them. Was he searching for some kind of latch, she wondered? But then she heard a soft click and the whole wall swung slowly outwards.

Fritz hurriedly stepped aside and stretched out his hand.

"Ladies first," he said meekly.

"Oh, no." Holly glared at him. "I insist."

They carefully alighted the cabin. It shook precariously as they left, and Holly wouldn't have been at all surprised if it chose that moment to go crashing back down into the Workers' District. She felt a weight lift from herself, too, and had to remind herself that their newfound 'solid' ground was still on board a space station hurtling its way through an orbit around Saturn.

The small room that welcomed them was brilliantly, almost uncomfortably white. You could get snow blindness from spending too long in it. There was no sign of the cobwebs and dust bunnies that plagued the sectors below, nor of any muck and grit brushed into hard-to-reach corners. Well, not anymore. The two of them were leaving grubby footprints everywhere they went.

If that continued for much longer, Holly thought, they might need to consider going barefoot. They couldn't afford to leave any clues behind.

Fritz nodded to a white door opposite. Its silver knob was the only object of note in the room. Holly nodded in return, and he slowly twisted it.

Holly expected a number of things. First and foremost, an angry horde of bloodthirsty killers wielding spanners and hatchets and table legs who'd been patiently awaiting their arrival. In addition to that, perhaps a direct line of sight with the welcome lobby and the security team's shuttle. Maybe even a view of the founders' heavenly utopia, with all the glitz and glam and tropical palm trees she envisioned.

A department store was not one of those things.

"Father O'Brien's tunnel leads into a fucking *Macey's?*" she asked.

"The elevator can go only go into what's directly above it," Fritz replied matter-of-factly. "What did you expect, a secret compartment to rise out of the public fountain?"

"No, it's just..." She gave up. "I guess I didn't realise the priest was in the market for designer robes."

Holly had never actually been inside a department store – not one still operating as anything other than an emergency shelter, anyway – but she'd seen old pictures and walked the modest commercial district of her Ark ship prior to settling on New Terra. This place looked like it was torn straight from the archives. Square pens of glass-topped counters. Rack upon rack of tuxedos, fur coats, sequinned dresses. Floor to ceiling mirrors framed in gold. Portraits of glamorous models encased in perspex. Impossibly polished floors. Soft-light chandeliers and intricate architecture inspired by classical-era cultures. Everything doused with irritating quantities of perfume and cologne.

Forget Macey's. Saturnalia gave Harrods a run for its money.

The rear of the door through which they entered was marked PRIVATE. It was next to a series of changing cubicles, each of which was adorned with ruby curtains so fine they'd make a theatre jealous. Someone had left a top hat on one of the stools inside.

"I thought you said this would get us closer to the shuttle," Holly said.

"Yes, *closer*. But not as close as the maintenance elevator would have taken us."

"Well, which way is it to the atrium?"

Fritz stared at her blankly.

"How should I know?" he hissed. "Do you think I come in here to shop once a week, or something? The last time I was out and about inside the Residential District... well, it was pretty much when I first got here!"

Holly ground her teeth together.

"You said you could show me the way!"

"Yes, and I can figure out the rest once we're somewhere I recognise. But that doesn't mean I somehow know my way around the shopping district—"

Rapid footsteps coming their way. Fritz grabbed Holly and pulled her down behind a display counter full of glittery rings and necklaces worth more than she could hope to make in a lifetime.

Through the sparkling glass she watched as a distressed woman in a pencil-dress sprinted through the aisles of the department store, passing only a coat rack's distance from their hiding place.

"Please, leave me alone," she cried. "I want nothing to do with you!"

Two men chased after her. Holly ducked further down. Fritz had his back to the display case. One of the men wore a ripped version of the same navy blue overalls Fritz had on; the other, a blood-stained combo of dark green shirt and trousers. A former custodian, perhaps.

Their footsteps echoed more and more quietly, and then all was silent again. Holly waited for a high-pitched scream. She was left waiting, thankfully. She hoped the poor woman had been able to escape the men, as unlikely as it seemed.

"Did you see them?" she asked Fritz, knowing he'd been facing the other way. "That woman was definitely upper crust. And the men chasing her looked like they, well... like they worked downstairs with you."

"So?"

"The people trying to kill us downstairs – they looked like residents, I think. But those men just now were workers. Whatever kind of civil war happened here, Fritz, I don't think the wealthy won. Or at least, I don't think *anyone* did. Maybe the survivors are just going around hunting down whoever's left, regardless of where they came from."

"Whatever." Fritz shrugged and peered around the edge of the display case. "I don't care why this happened, or who's fighting who. I just want off this station."

"Yeah, I suppose someone's reasons don't mean much when they're putting a screwdriver through your skull. We ought to get moving before anyone comes back. How do we get out of here, do you think?"

They squinted each way. In one direction, a lot of shoes. In the other, designer handbags. The pillars of the hall stretched on and on.

"That's the thing about these posh places," Fritz grumbled. "They make the signs less obvious. Keeps you inside so you spend more."

Holly tried to use the layout of the Workers' District to orient herself. If the church was directly beneath them, and the laundry room was that way, then...

"I reckon the exit is somewhere over there," she whispered, jabbing a hand in the direction ahead of them. "Or we'll be closer to it, at any rate."

"Your guess is as good as mine," Fritz said resignedly.

Crouched over like crabs, they crept across the hall towards the handbags. One display was packed with leathery clutches. Holly was tempted to grab a few of the smaller items, or to slip her arms through one of the fur-lined coats. If she made it back to New Terra in one piece, she could make a fortune.

They kept going, sticking to the featured displays and pillars, disguising themselves amongst the merchandise whenever possible. They heard the occasional shout but saw no-one. When they hit a tiled perimeter wall modelled on an Egyptian temple, they amended their trajectory by ninety degrees and found themselves in a section marked NIGHTWEAR.

"Explain to me how any of this makes sense," Holly whispered to Fritz as they ducked behind a display of lingerie. "The founders spent enormous fortunes on creating Saturnalia. Their residency here, and the residency of their children, is set for life. All the food and service and enter-tainment is bought and paid for. So why the hell do they need a shopping district?"

"They're rich," Fritz replied, distracted. "Rich people like buying things."

"But they're *not* buying things! They're pretending to peruse things the Flynn Industries fund has already bought for them! This place is nothing but a... a walk-in catalogue of products they already own. It's weird."

"I suppose they..." Fritz shook his head clear. "Do you want a full breakdown of Saturnalia's economy, or do you want to get off this station in one piece?"

"It's just so fake, that's all."

"And the people we're talking about aren't?"

They paused as a wave of shrieking laughter swept down from the floor overhead. Shadows as thin as fish knives stabbed across the wall above the nearby escalators, flickered back and forth like candle flames. Holly gripped the plastic shelves of the gridwall tight, ready to run, but the shadows grew thinner, paler, and then vanished.

Turning to leave, Holly almost let out a shriek of her own. For a split second she truly believed death was inches away. But it was only a naked mannequin that stood behind her, its dainty hand raised to the heavens in a delicate salute. She shook her head, embarrassed and disappointed with herself.

"I'm losing my fucking marbles," she muttered.

Clothing gave way to household goods. Photo frames with inlaid jewellery. Potted plants (to be watered by housekeeping, of course). Hand-carved side tables and plush office armchairs. There were even a few marble statues on plinths, though it was sometimes difficult to tell what was on sale and what belonged to the department store's over-dramatic decor.

These things she could understand. Of course the residents would want to redecorate their suites as the years went by.

It was the section marked HOUSEKEEPING that bothered her.

"But they don't *do* any housekeeping," she said through gritted teeth as they passed a podium of vacuum cleaners torn straight from a 1950s brochure. "They don't even have half of this stuff in their apartments, right? I mean, why would you want a rumbly old washing machine taking up space when you're paying someone else to wash your dirties for you?"

"Nope," Fritz said, glancing over his shoulder. "The maids bring the housekeeping equipment with them and take all the laundry away. And all the cooking on Saturnalia is done inside the restaurant and canteen kitchens. And that's not just because most of the residents have never held so much as a spatula in their lives. It's too dangerous to use gas and open flames – even electric stoves – outside of sealable compartments."

"Then why," Holly said, tapping a knuckle against the side of a spotless tumble dryer that could well have begun life during the Kennedy administration, "is there a whole section of this department store dedicated to selling these rich bastards a load of white goods?"

Fritz hesitated.

"Maria always said that half of the stuff in this store was just for display. Of course the residents don't actually *want* to buy a washing machine – they already paid for the industrial cleaners downstairs. And it's not like any of them would ever come into this section to browse anything, either. They just want the *impression* of realness, of everything being just the same as it was back on Earth, you know?"

"Back on Earth? Were these people *ever* close enough to the ground to know what real life was like? There hasn't been a place like this for the best part of half a century. And look at all these relics. It's not just pre-Exodus. This is from before they were born."

"I don't think it's nostalgia for a time they knew," Fritz said dismissively, "but a time they consider… better. Where, you know, everybody knew their place. Now *shh*. Look over there."

Holly struggled to figure out what Fritz wanted her to see. A giant bronze statue stood in the centre of an open roundabout of customer pathways next to—

The exit. Bright sunlight – well, bright *artificial* sunlight – bled in from the promenade outside. Ruby-coloured ropes lined the aisle leading from the open doorway to the statue as if to keep the riff-raff at bay, and a delicate stream trickled down the five slanted rocks of an elaborate water feature set to one side.

There were no shutters with which to lock up the store come closing time, Holly noticed. With the rich getting whatever they wanted, and with the poor having nowhere to hide, she supposed there really wasn't much incentive to steal anything.

"—almost the last of them," said a scratchy voice from outside the store as its owner grew closer. "Just a few camped out in the play-house, and then..."

Shit. As the layout of the department store grew more sparse, so did decent places to hide. Holly crouched behind a large rubber-plant in a terracotta pot (and it really *was* rubber, she quickly realised upon closer inspection) while Fritz stood out in the open like an embarrassed scarecrow before darting behind the bronze statue. Neither of them were particularly well hidden.

"Did you hear about the stowaways they found down-stairs?" the scratchy-voiced man asked his companion as they entered. "Corey got 'em in the EVA pod."

They took a right at the statue. Fritz shut his eyes and grimaced.

"I heard she took out all of Laundry doing it," the other man replied haughtily. "Serves those heretics right, though. May their corpses lie frozen and forgotten for eternity..."

So, they think we're dead, Holly thought to herself. Good. That's one advantage, at least.

The two men laughed and slapped one another on the back as they strolled towards the section of the store marked ELECTRONICS. Fritz slowly and painfully manoeuvred his way around the statue as they disappeared around the corner, keeping it between them and him, locking eyes with Holly the whole time.

He nodded pointedly to the exit. Holly raised her eyebrows and widened her eyes in agreement. He snuck out via the empty aisle; she ducked under the security banner and then threw herself against the wall outside.

The exterior that greeted her was no less confounding.

"Erm, Fritz?" she whispered. "Are you sure we're in the right place? Hell, are you sure we're in the right *time*?"

"Forget about the real world," he replied, dragging her away from the store's entrance. "You're in Saturnalia now."

CHAPTER
THIRTEEN

I t wasn't real.

Of course, nothing was. Saturnalia was a luxury space station housing the richest of the rich, people so elevated from normal reality that they quite literally floated above a gas giant. Hell, they weren't even in the same *star system* as everybody else. You expected some degree of show-manship to the surroundings in order to convince everyone on board they were somewhere safe and familiar and opulent and not trapped inside a tiny aluminium can that could be punctured at any moment.

But... *it wasn't real.*

There'd been theme parks in the early twenty-first century less artificial than this. Holly wasn't convinced that anywhere on Earth had *ever* resembled the Main Street of Saturnalia's Residential District. Not unless you counted the sets from half a dozen different movies from Hollywood's Golden Age. This was the product of pure imagination, through and through.

The street itself – if a stretch of road that had never seen an automobile in its life could be called a street, that is – was covered in cobbles, as if lifted from an old Dickensian novel. Street lamps lined the pavements, which hardly seemed necessary given the aforementioned lack of vehicles, and were also designed to resemble those of Victorian London. Black metal pillars with squiggly iron bits from the top of which three glass lanterns sprouted, each housing a bulb fashioned to look like a gas flame. Holly didn't know what time it was on the station, but right now they were switched off.

The walls of Main Street ran perfectly parallel to one another and were covered in pretend apartment buildings. Not that she'd ever had the fortune to visit, but, having read a few history books, she believed the architecture intended to ape that of Paris, with intricate stonework and iron grates across the balcony windows. It was undeniably beautiful, and the fake blue-grey rooftops cute and quirky, but it was obvious nobody lived behind their two-dimensional curtains. They were about as convincing as the ceiling, which was painted a perfect sky blue with sporadic tufts of white cloud added for effect. But she suspected nobody expected them to undergo serious scrutiny.

Running along the bottom storey of all these 'buildings' were actual stores, or at least the façades of sets masquerading as them. Behind Holly and Fritz stood Harringdon's, the department store that dominated one end of the street. The enormous letters of its name were bolted into the stonework above the doorway. The rest were mostly smaller establishments. Many of their front windows had been smashed in the riots, and their wares lay sprawled out across the cobbles... as did a couple of dead shopkeepers, too. Stale doughnuts and mouldy croissants identified a bakery; while Holly had no doubt the residents enjoyed the occasional muffin or cupcake, and the bakery probably had a standing order for various residents' birthday cakes, its primary purpose was likely to fill the promenade with the smell of freshly baked bread each morning. Beside this was a brick-and-mortar bookstore, or possibly some kind of high-end library, and next to that the sort of boutique coffee shop even the valley girls of California would have found too pretentious. But the most bizarre inclusion had to be the shop selling wedding dresses. How many of Saturnalia's residents had a regular need for *that*?

Holly stopped short opposite an ice cream parlour. She grabbed the shoulder of Fritz's overalls and nodded feverishly towards its open doorway. An older gentleman in light blue medical scrubs had his back to them, a child's doll cradled in his arms, and was rocking back and forth in front of a giant sign shaped like a strawberry sundae with chocolate drizzle and a cherry on top.

"They want to take it away from me," he was muttering to himself. "I won't *let* them take it away from me..."

Holly and Fritz shared a disturbed look. He raised a finger to his lips, and they quickly crept further along the pavement until both the man and his ice cream parlour were out of sight.

Save for the rocking man and the pair of corpses, Main Street was deserted – certainly now that the other two locals had wandered into the department store. It looked as if the other end of the street had suffered the worst of the uprising, with some of the fake frontage actually pulled free from its industrial supports behind, but for now everything was quiet.

Almost eerily so. It was disconcerting how quickly one got used to the mechanical *clinks* and *clanks* of the lower levels.

Fritz took her by the hand and hauled her towards a

semi-circular fabric marquee jutting out between two store-fronts. Holly shook her head in continuing disbelief at every establishment they passed. The only thing missing from this picture was a goddamn horse-drawn carriage.

There had to be a word to describe nostalgia for a time and place which had never actually existed, let alone been experienced by anyone, but she wasn't aware of one. Perhaps 'Saturnalia Syndrome' would suffice going forward.

Trees alternated with the street lamps along both pavements. Fritz pulled her into the shade of one with a particularly heavy canopy and frantically looked up and down the promenade, then under the classy overhang. A rustic wooden signpost stood in the centre of the street. Holly read the words stencilled onto its three arms: HARRINGDON'S, SUITES and ATRIUM.

"This is the tunnel that leads back to the welcome lobby," Fritz whispered to her, peering down the fateful corridor. "It's a straight shot, but if we get caught in there, we're screwed."

"You don't have to tell me," Holly sighed. "This is where my security team got killed. And there's no better way through?"

"Not that I know of. Sorry."

"It's fine." Holly pursed her lips. "We'd have to step out into the open in order to board the shuttle, anyway."

"It's clear." Fritz was sweating profusely again. "Should we go?"

Holly hesitated, her fingers on one hand tapping out a nervous rhythm against the knuckles of her other. She glanced back at the department store, then up towards the residential apartments. God, it was tempting to leave, to cut her losses and call it quits.

"Not yet," she said determinedly. "I still need to find Mrs. Flynn."

"Are you...?" Fritz lowered his voice. "Are you fucking *kidding* me? You're still going on about that shit? I get that you thought rescuing this woman was possible before. I mean, I saved you, right? But we almost died in Laundry, Holly. They vented a whole section of the station just to get at us! Mrs. Flynn is dead. Let her go."

"You don't know that. What about your wife? Are you giving up on her, too?"

"Don't you..." Fritz huffed. "Yes, I thought there was a chance when we got back to my quarters. I'll admit it. But I was stupid. Look at the lengths they're going to, hunting down survivors. She's as dead as that rich bitch of yours, and we both know it."

Holly felt hot rage build inside of her. They might both be scared shitless, but there was no need for comments like that.

"There's even the slightest chance Maria is alive somewhere on Saturnalia, and you're willing to leave her behind to save your own skin? Bullshit. Doesn't add up. What aren't you telling me, Fritz?"

"What the hell are you on about?"

"I saw her picture in your quarters, sure. You *were* married, I'll believe that. But maybe she never made it to Saturnalia in the first place. Maybe that's why you're in such a hurry to leave."

Fritz stared at her in blank disbelief.

"You're a real piece of fucking work, Holly, you know that? Come on, then. Let's hear your plan. People who've lived on this station for years have been hunting down survivors for the past three days, but you – a woman who couldn't even find her way out of Engineering on her own, remember? – are going to somehow find this Flynn woman's as-of-yet undiscovered hiding spot before they do and then escort her back to the shuttle without anyone noticing? Please, out with it. This is going to be good."

Holly bit her lip hard enough to draw blood. Once again, the coward was right. If Rosie Flynn *had* survived this long, it was because she couldn't be found... and not for lack of trying.

"Shit."

"Yeah, I thought so. Shit indeed. You're an analyst, Holly, not a soldier. You can't help her. The best thing we can do is get on that shuttle and send an urgent message to Flynn Industries, or the goddamn UEC, en route to New Terra. If Maria and Mrs. Flynn *are* still alive, a platoon of marines is going to do a much better job at saving them than the two of us. And you heard those guys talking in the store. Right now, they think we're dead. Let's keep it that way."

"Fine. Yes." She buried her head in her hands and groaned. "Argh. I can't believe I flew a dozen lightyears for this mess. Screw it. Let's get out of here."

"I wouldn't worry yourself too much," Fritz said spitefully. "I'm sure you'll still get paid."

With the tunnel leading to the atrium still clear, they quickly hurried down its length. Holly could already see the brass railing of the balcony on the other side, and the benches – like that of an old-fashioned railway station, she remembered – and the twinkling tip of the grand chandelier a little past that. Even as escape beckoned, her stomach grew tighter. She felt like vomiting. To come all this way, only to turn tail and run back home...

It made sense, but it hurt like hell to admit it.

"The pilots," Fritz hissed as they approached the end of the tunnel. "They'll know who you are, right?"

"Erm, good point."

Had either of the pilots actually seen her during the flight at all? Nobody had gone up or down the ladder that led to the cockpit save for when Carlson went to check on comms prior to docking. She tried to recall their names, but couldn't.

"I'm sure they'll recognise me," she bluffed. "Especially if I namedrop the security team. It'll be fine."

But the further down the tunnel they got, the more her gut told her it wouldn't. Because while she couldn't remember either of the pilots' names, she *did* recall a comment Carlson had made to them shortly before being bludgeoned to death.

Don't let anyone on board the ship without my clearance.

Well, she sure as shit didn't have that. What *was* his clearance, anyway? An abstract acknowledgement given only to the sergeant of a fireteam? Or a physical keycard or other such gizmo, without which you couldn't open the shuttle door?

The pilots would ignore the order, she decided. They had to. The security team was dead and the station overrun with murderers. This was no time to worry about official protocol.

Blood stains on the floor. Not just blood, either. Brains and shards of bone, too. The bodies of the security team had been moved – dragged, by the looks of it. Maybe they were somewhere close, she suddenly thought. Maybe, if they hadn't been robbed of their belongings, she could find this 'clearance' and—

"Oh God," Fritz moaned, covering his mouth as they reached the end of the tunnel. He turned away. "Please tell me that's not your team…"

Five bodies hung from the rafters around the chandelier,

frayed nooses wrapped around their necks. It would have been six, but one of the bodies had suffered such horrific trauma to the head that it had slipped through the rope and splattered against the polished marble tiles of the atrium below. Illegible scrawls were painted in blood across each victim's uniform.

From left to right: Wade, Lynch, Banks (he was the smear on the floor, she guessed), Carlson, and then...

"No, no, *no*," Holly cried. She collapsed onto the closest bench on the balcony. "The pilots. They killed the pilots, too."

It wasn't that she could identify them, as such. She hadn't seen their faces, which were certainly too bloated and purple to recognise now, anyway. Putting aside a basic process of elimination – who else were they going to be, really? – their pale grey flight uniforms gave them away. And the doors of the airlock beneath their dangling feet were busted wide open on both sides. After killing the security team, the locals must have somehow forced their way through the docking tunnel and dragged the poor pilots out.

Damn fools. They should have headed straight back to New Terra the moment they saw maniacs hammering on the airlock's exterior. She guessed they didn't want to be responsible for spacing a bunch of old toffs who were off their meds.

Well, now they were dead, and Holly was stuck on Saturnalia with no hope of escape.

"We should have known they wouldn't let an outsider's shuttle just sit idle out there for long," Fritz sighed. "This was a stupid plan from the start. *Stupid*."

He brightened suddenly.

"Wait – what if *we* flew the ship?" he said, crouching

beside her. "It's probably still docked with the station, right? Let's take it!"

"Are you mad?" Holly teetered on the verge of hysterics. "What makes you think either one of us can operate a shuttle like that? I don't even have a driver's license. We wouldn't know how to close the bloody door, let alone disengage from the station and launch the thrusters. And even if we *did* get it going, do you know how to get to New Terra from here? We'd fly it into a fucking sun, Fritz."

"Yeah." He deflated. "Yeah, I guess you're right. So, that's it, then? We find somewhere to hole up and hope Flynn Industries sends another security team."

"Nobody else will get here for at least another few days. And they'll likely just assume our lack of contact is down to a bigger issue with the comms relay than originally thought. Unless..."

She pulled Fritz close.

"You're an electrical engineer, right? So you could fix the comms issue?"

"I mean, it's not my precise area of expertise," he said, prying his overalls free from Holly's grip. "But sure, I could give it a shot. Of course, it *could* be a mechanical fault..."

"We'll worry about that later. We start by diagnosing the problem – then we figure out a way to fix it. Okay. This is good. What do you need to make this happen?"

"What do I need?" Fritz blew a raspberry. "Access to Administration, for a start. That's where all inter-system communication gets sent. Can't say more until I know what we're dealing with, though."

A natural contractor, Holly thought.

"And how do we get you there?"

"I mean, the quickest way is up through the Residential Suites. But that place is gonna be crawling with—"

Two women and a man kicked open the door to the security office and spilled into the atrium. Holly and Fritz ducked behind the bench. The intruders were smiling in their deranged, carved-into-their-face kind of way, but it was clear something had caught their attention.

"Am I right in guessing there are cameras on this station?" Holly whispered urgently.

"Of course," he replied with dawning horror. "Everywhere public, that is."

"Then we ought to get moving, fast." She pulled Fritz back towards the corridor. "The suites are our best bet. That's as private as it gets. The fewer eyes on us, the better."

They dashed back towards Main Street before the killers could climb the stairs.

Back to Plan A it is, then. Fix the comms issue, and bring the full might of the UEC down on this madhouse.

CHAPTER
FOURTEEN

Main Street remained deserted. The same classical piano music playing perpetually in the atrium was also piped through here, but now that Holly noticed it she realised the track was slowing down and lowering in pitch, as if the wax of the vinyl record were melting.

She double checked the decorative wooden signpost. Its overly embellished arm pointing to the right read SUITES. They followed it.

The speakers hidden in the façades weren't the only things failing. One of the lights nestled amongst Main Street's rooftops cut out, spluttered out some nonsense in morse code, and then reluctantly returned to life. Water trickled through the open door of the coffee shop and transformed the cobbles outside into an orderly archipelago.

A series of ominous clunking sounds ran down the length of the promenade's painted ceiling. Fritz stopped walking and listened with a growing expression of concern.

"The station is starting to lose power," he mumbled. "Things will begin to shut down, sector by sector."

"Will we run out of air?"

"Life-support systems will be the last to go," Fritz replied, shaking his head without much conviction. "There's always plenty of juice in reserve in case the generators die. It won't last forever, though."

"How long?"

"A few days? If the population of Saturnalia has been drastically reduced, maybe as long as a week." He shrugged. "I don't think it's something we've tested."

"So we'd better get that message out to Flynn Industries," Holly said, continuing her trek down the street. "Even if the remaining survivors manage to stay hidden, they'll suffocate to death if we don't get things under control."

"As will we," Fritz reminded her.

Heated conversation from back in the tunnel. They darted inside the nearest store and hid behind the low walls of its street-facing windows. The bottom half of the glass had been painted in bright colours. Holly didn't think they'd been spotted, but the three people in the atrium had burst out from the security office. She and Fritz could have been caught on camera. Hell, somebody could be watching the two of them *right now*.

Holly ducked down further as the same group from earlier strolled past the windows. It looked like they were headed for the Residential Suites as well. They still wore mad grins as fake as Main Street, but Holly felt some measure of relief that they didn't appear to be on the hunt for anyone in particular.

Or perhaps they just weren't in any rush. With the pilots dead, nobody was going anywhere.

Holly sank down with her back against the wall. A fresh itch crept over her skin as she realised where she was hiding.

Bean bag chairs and plastic stools made up most of the room's furniture. Overlapping hills of green felt formed a 3D landscape along the right-hand wall. Children's drawings had been pinned to it. Soft balls and plastic trains spilled out of an overturned toy box. Retro videogame consoles and arcade machines from before even Holly's time lined the rear of the room, as did an array of television screens.

"Erm, Fritz? Is this some kind of daycare centre?"

"Yes," he replied, giving the room only the most cursory of glances as he scanned the street for more killers. "A handful of residents had small children with them when they arrived. Often the infant grandchildren of the original founders."

He suppressed a cough. It sounded as if something had caught in his throat.

"Not the workers, mind you." There was no mistaking the bitterness in his voice, even if he tried to act like he was just making polite conversation. "It wasn't that reproduction was explicitly banned, as such, but... well, it would have been a really stupid idea. No support, no money, no food for you or the baby... and no free ride back to New Terra, either. Good thing Maria and I were too old for all that nonsense, anyway."

Holly decided not to wade back into the murky waters of Saturnalia's employee rights. It sounded appropriately awful, and Fritz didn't just know it – he'd lived it.

"How many children?" she asked, finding it difficult to swallow.

"Here? Oh, not many. Six, maybe? No more than eight."

"And where are they now?"

His attention finally torn from the windows, Fritz gave the nursery a mournful look.

"Somewhere safe, I hope," he said.

Holly found herself incapable of moving, feeling – anything. She knew she should be hiding behind the cases full of children's books in the event that one of the crazy locals walked back down Main Street and happened to glance inside the daycare centre, but she didn't care. She *couldn't* care. Her mortal body may have been standing inside that room, but she was long, *long* gone, falling deep into the blackness, the light from outside her eyes mere pinpricks – two faint stars alone in the cosmos.

It wasn't even the prospect of murdered kids that had rattled her, though she truly hoped somebody had thought to hide them when the violence first broke out. No, this dread took root long before Saturnalia. The sight of soft toys and unintelligible doodles had unexpectedly transported her back to the living room in her family photograph.

She could almost see her sister, still so young she was wearing nothing but a diaper, crawl across the nursery floor in front of her. Her parents sat and watched from the plastic stools, arms wrapped around each other, laughing as if the world wasn't burning outside... as if any of them still had a future together.

Lies, all of it. Of that once perfect, happy family, Holly was all that remained.

"Holly?" Fritz shook her gently by the shoulder. "Street's clear. We've gotta go."

"Yeah." Holly followed him out, though she was too numb to feel her legs walking. "Yeah, all right."

They lingered together in the doorway, Fritz checking up and down the street while Holly fought to break free from her disassociation. Then they sprinted towards the end of Main Street, as far from the Harringdon's department store as one could go. Holly paid no mind to the empty stores and boutiques and blank façades that passed by to either side of them, nor to the bodies and blood that may or may not have darkened their doorways. She needed to keep it together. One bad move – a single momentary lapse of judgement – and they'd be just another pair of corpses sprawled across the cobbles.

The entrance to the suites was located a short distance past a Japanese cherry blossom tree. Given that it was in full bloom, Holly assumed it was artificial – just like everything else on the station. The street curved around it in a circle like the driveway of a manor house.

It was the only building not to fit in with the pseudo-Parisian theme, though, as with everything else on Main Street, it was just a front. With hundreds of residents occupying Saturnalia, there was no way the four-storey building before her could accommodate everyone. The real complex stretched much further back, outwards and upwards than the two-dimensional frontage suggested. It was meticulously detailed, ostentatious in its contrast with everything else, and extravagantly art deco. Myriad narrow windows – pretend, of course – lined the upper floors. A fan of decorative gold plates was installed above the entrance, and an array of spotlights spread their beams across the sand-brown stonework in a similar peacocking display. And the rooftop rose to a narrow point in emulation of old New York skyscrapers.

Well, she couldn't blame them. If she had paid billions of dollars to build a super-deluxe space station, she wouldn't want to feel as if she were living above the local deli, either.

Ensuring they were hidden behind the plush cherry blossom petals before taking a moment to catch their breath, Holly and Fritz scrutinised the way forward.

"Well, how the hell are we supposed to get through that?" Holly asked, exasperated.

Two short sets of stone steps flanked a disabled-access ramp, which connected the suites' big, brass doorway to Main Street. Two stone pillars topped with lion statues stood to either side of a large, spiked gate. Who the residents thought they were keeping out under normal circumstances was anybody's guess, and Holly supposed it, like most things, was really only for show. But not only was it now padlocked shut, but all manner of different cables and brooms and crowbars had been threaded and speared through its iron poles. Trying to squeeze through would more likely result in mild impalement.

"I don't suppose you happen to have a spare key, do you?" she asked Fritz.

"We could try to climb over the fence to either side," he suggested.

"Using what? I don't see any handholds. And even if we could, look how sharp those spikes are. They might be the only thing on this station that *is* real."

They froze as somebody crossed the street about thirty metres behind them. A woman from the earlier patrol, Holly reckoned. She disappeared into the nursery from which they just left.

They needed to hurry.

"Shit." Holly chewed her lip as she tried – and failed – to imagine another way around. "This is a lost cause already. We need to go back."

"Not necessarily." Fritz nodded to the Haussmann-inspired townhouse next door to the suites. "See that store there? That's the pharmacy."

She could see that. It had a green plus sign hanging from the front and everything.

"So?"

"So that's where Dr. Humphreys lives. Or lived, I guess. He was the primary physician here as well as the pharmacist. Cared for the rich and workers alike. And with so many of the residents getting on in years, he must have been popping in and out of the suites with their medication all the time. I bet he has another way of getting inside."

"Could be more discreet, too," Holly said, hurriedly glancing back down Main Street. "All right, then. Let's try it."

They left the shadow of the tree and crept next door. The door to the pharmacy hadn't been busted open, but it was unlocked. It let out a quiet creak as it swung inwards. Holly and Fritz slipped in silently and closed it behind them.

It was dark inside; though it wasn't fake like those of the upper storeys, the heavily frosted glass of the pharmacy's lone window let in little of the light from Main Street. The residents presumably wanted a degree of privacy if they were paying Dr. Humphreys a visit. Fluorescent strips were embedded in the ceiling, but flicking the light switch inside the doorway did nothing. Either the electrics were faulty or the good doctor had, for some unfathomable reason, removed all of the bulbs.

The pharmacy reminded Holly of the infirmaries back when she'd been growing up on Earth, and then, years later, on board the Ark ship. Fortunately, she'd always been blessed with good health, and the strong smell of antiseptic was not one to which her nose was particularly accustomed. There wasn't much in the way of a waiting room, with only a pair of plush armchairs for visiting residents to sit in and a fairly anonymous print of a farmhouse hanging on the nondescript wall. The rest of the room was occupied by a beige counter. Behind that were stacks of the most popular medicines – painkillers such as paracetamol and ibuprofen, melatonin and other sleeping aids, and an array of allergy tablets – and through a heavily fortified (though currently wide open) door like that of a safe lay the rest of the pharmaceuticals. It was surely only a matter of time before the more unhinged residents decided to plunder the horde of fentanyl and diamorphine inside.

With no sign of Humphreys's body, nor of any way into the suites from inside the pharmacy itself, they continued past the waiting room and down a narrow corridor. It went on for quite some distance, and Holly was beginning to think they might already be inside the apartment building when they passed the doorway of Saturnalia's operating theatre.

There had to be one, of course, and she imagined there were even better equipped versions hidden elsewhere around the station in case of emergencies. A whole minia-ture hospital of surgeons and nurses permanently on standby, no doubt, given the importance of the clientele. Humphreys was just the friendly face of healthcare on board Saturnalia, the general practitioner. Somebody had be on call for when the older residents fell or developed arthritis or Alzheimers. But there were accidents, too, not to mention cancers and strokes and other unpredictable illnesses that arrived upon the roll of a die. It would have been damn poor luck to travel all this way across the stars and then die from something as mundane and avoidable as radiation poison-ing. Or gout.

In the centre of the room was an operating table – beside it, a small, wheeled tray containing an assortment of scalpels and tweezers and scissors. Against the wall to the right of this was an industrial sink, a soap dispenser, and two bins for the recycling and disposal of gowns and gloves. The rear wall, opposite the doorway in which Holly stood, was lined with shelves decked with all manner of different chemical bottles. Lastly, some kind of white, glossy incubation pod for adults was pushed up against the left-hand wall beside a large refrigeration unit. Like the rooms in the workers' canteen, the floor was fitted with a round, grated drain for washing away spillages.

Holly was about to continue down the corridor when a sudden stab of pain ran from her wrist to her elbow. She paused by the doorway to prod gingerly at the cut on her arm.

"You're hurt," Fritz said, doubling back. "Let me take a look at it."

"What are you, a doctor all of a sudden?"

"No, but I've seen my fair share of injuries in my time. Been on the receiving end of a few, too."

Holly's sleeve had slipped down; she rolled it back up to her elbow and winced as Fritz unravelled her makeshift bandage. The dirty blue fabric she borrowed from Engineering was now a red-brown colour.

Yeah, the cut didn't look so good.

"It's going to get infected," Fritz said frankly. Holly thought he could work on his bedside manner. "The pills you need are probably here somewhere, but you'd need a doctor to tell you which ones."

"Well, isn't that some perfect irony."

"We ought to clean it out, anyway. Stop it from getting any worse."

Holly followed him into the operating room. She briefly considered hopping up onto the table like a patient, then thought better of it. It didn't look clean. Her clothes may have already been drenched in her own blood, but that didn't mean she needed to add somebody else's to the mix.

Fritz perused the shelves for a moment, then hurried back clutching one of the bottles.

He opened it, gave it a sniff, then shook his head clear of the pungent odour inside.

"Surgical spirit," he said, catching Holly's worried look.

"I'd rather it was gin," she replied, holding out her arm. "And this'll help, will it?"

"It can't hurt, can it?" Fritz went to pour, then paused. "That's not true. It'll hurt quite a bit. But it's definitely better than leaving the wound to fester any further. Ready?"

"Do it."

He gently splashed the bottle's contents over the cut on her arm. She drew a sharp intake of breath through her gritted teeth. Fuck, that stung. It felt like Fritz had stuck a fire iron in there.

"Here," he said, first using a towelette to dab away the runoff and then awkwardly handing it to her to finish the job.

"Thanks," she replied, patting her arm dry. Fritz once again disappeared towards the drawers behind her. This time he returned with a white gauze bandage, which she used to finally dress the wound properly. "Will I lose it, Doc?"

Fritz smiled politely.

"Rest here for a second. I'll have a look for that shortcut into the suites."

"Nonsense. I haven't been maimed, Fritz."

"No, but you can afford to let your arm stop aching for a few minutes. Besides, we might not know what antibiotics you need, but you can bet your ass there's a tonne of painkillers here. Grab a packet or two. I've got a headache that needs getting rid of as well."

Holly sighed. Her arm did still sting something fierce,

and there wasn't much benefit to be gained from both of them crowding into the doctor's quarters.

"Fine. But hurry back. This place gives me the creeps."

Fritz lingered in the doorway.

"And the rest of the station doesn't?" he muttered sarcastically before disappearing into the corridor.

CHAPTER FIFTEEN

The rest of the corridor was just as narrow and twice as dark. There was only just enough room to walk in single file, and the light from Main Street couldn't permeate this far into the pharmacy. From somewhere inside the walls came a weird, repetitive scratching sound, like cogs that had got caught.

Fritz edged onwards, his jaw clenched as tightly as his fists. He wished he'd brought the bottle of surgical spirit with him. If anyone pounced out, he could smash it over their head.

He thought back to his tools, lost somewhere down in Engineering. Alas, if only he still had his socket wrench...

A soft glow emanated from somewhere past the end of the corridor, bathing its conclusion in what amounted to little more than candlelight. Fritz hoped it wasn't a candle – any open flame outside of the kitchens could prove catastrophic, and even then he'd always wished the chefs would just keep any dish that needed flambéing off the menu. At least the smell of antiseptic hand wash had subsided a little.

He reached the junction. To the right, another dark tunnel. Fritz felt optimistic; it reminded him of the access and service corridors. To the left, a short flight of stairs leading to the floor above. It was from up there that both the meagre light and the odd scratching noise originated.

Glancing back down the corridor to the almost moonlit doorway of the operating room in which Holly waited with her convalescent arm, he decided to take a look upstairs. That wound would need a pair of qualified eyes cast over it sooner or later, and Humphreys had always been good to Maria on the odd occasion when she'd taken ill. Plus, this place hadn't been ransacked yet. If the doctor was hiding upstairs, maybe the two of them could get him to safety, too.

He tiptoed up the carpeted steps.

Old-world photographs hung from the wall of the stairwell. Fritz recognised a younger Dr. Humphreys in a few of them. He presumed others were memories of partners and family members now lost, and cursed himself for not thinking to grab the photo of him and Maria from the small picture frame back in his quarters.

The door at the top of the stairs was already open. The wallpaper in the stairwell (or printed panels designed to resemble wallpaper, at any rate) continued into the room beyond, and through the doorway Fritz spotted an antique lamp shade jutting out from the wall. The bright light of the lightbulb was muted by its tasselled, orange fabric.

He cautiously peered further around the door frame, unsure if he could sprint back down the narrow stairs if he was spotted without tumbling and breaking his neck.

From what Maria had told Fritz about the suites, Dr. Humphrey's personal quarters weren't quite as fancy, but it was still a very nice apartment. Far more luxurious than anything found in the Workers' District, that was for sure. It was a benefit of being one of the more respected employees on board Saturnalia. The founders could afford to bring the best of the best with them from Earth. Andrew Yang, the administrator in charge of the station, and the various chefs of the Resort District had apartments like this, too.

The floor was carpeted just like the stairs, and a plush Persian rug stretched under much of the busy living room's furniture. Like the lamp shade by the door, most of the furnishings were either antique or designed to give that impression. The lone armchair was leather, its stuffing beginning to poke through the seams in a few places. There were no other chairs; Fritz guessed the doctor wasn't used to having visitors outside of his surgery. The walls were lined with bookcases whose shelves sagged under legions of hefty hardcovers. More framed photographs, plus a few small oil paintings. Through an archway to his left, Fritz spotted what amounted to Humphrey's kitchen. No actual cooking equipment, of course, but a sink and a small refrigerator, a similar table to that in Fritz's quarters, plus a reasonable amount of pantry space. A cold cup of tea and a plate of half-eaten biscuits had been left on the coffee table back in the living room.

Fritz discovered the source of the odd scratching noise. A vinyl had been playing on an old record player, and had since finished. The needle was carving a fresh groove through the dead wax next to the round label in the record's middle.

He quietly crossed to the other side of the apartment and lifted the needle free. The scratching stopped.

"Doctor Humphreys?" he whispered. He winced as the words broke the fresh silence. "Are you in here? It's Fritz Fredersen. I'm not like the others. I'm not here to hurt you."

He chastised himself. *I'm not here to hurt you.* Stupid.

That was exactly what one of those lunatics wandering through Engineering would say.

Another door was cracked ever so slightly open just past the kitchen's nook. A bedroom – Fritz could see the edge of a dresser through the gap. He formed a mental map of the apartment. Given where the sink had been installed... the pipework... yes, he reckoned there'd be an en suite with toilet and shower cubicle somewhere back there, too.

He looked around for a weapon, couldn't find anything more dangerous than one of Humphrey's dusty tomes, and gave up. At least this door was well-oiled enough not to creak as he slowly pushed it open.

"Ach du lieber..."

A body lay sprawled across the bedcovers of the double bed inside. Fritz was more surprised by his lack of revulsion than by the sight of the corpse itself. It was just one more dead body making a slow trip around Saturn, he supposed.

And the body was definitely dead. Had been for a few days, if Fritz had to guess. Dr. Humphreys had never been a slim man, but he was starting to bloat, and foam had bubbled up around his mouth. There was a rancid smell. Flies would have started bothering him had there been any aboard the station.

An empty pot of pills had rolled out of the doctor's hand onto the bedcovers. There was no use in Fritz checking its label – he wouldn't have understood what the man had taken, anyway. The point was, the doctor did. Humphreys must have seen the writing on the wall when the violence first broke out and decided to take his own life instead.

"Sorry, Dr. Humphreys," Fritz sighed, covering his mouth as the stench overwhelmed him. "It's a nicer way to go than letting the *Verrückten* get at you, I suppose."

He returned to the living room and, out of habit,

switched the record player off completely. There was only so much juice left on the station. With nowhere else in the apartment to explore, he concluded that if there was another way into the suites from here, their best bet would be the dark tunnel headed in the other direction.

One last glance into the bedroom. Fritz shook his head disappointedly.

It was time he got back to Holly with the good news.

Holly decided to stay inside the operating room. The pharmacy may have been a warmer, more welcoming environment, and much better stocked with painkillers, but she didn't want one of the locals to spot her shadow moving about behind the frosted windows.

That, and she didn't want to stray too far from Fritz. As ulcer-inducing as the man could be sometimes, it was nice having another sane person around. Now that the shuttle was a no-go, he didn't actually need her anymore. She was beginning to worry he'd figure this out and leave *her* behind.

She'd pulled open a few cupboards and drawers at random but found little in the way of tablets and pills. A few needles and ampoules, but she didn't fancy experimenting with anything she couldn't buy over the counter back on New Terra.

That said, she was flagging quite a bit. A shot of adrenaline wouldn't go amiss...

Her attention kept drifting to the shiny incubator. It reminded her of the sort newborn babies get put into, only expanded to fit an adult. The lid pried open on hydraulics like a tanning booth, and the 'bed' inside was lined with spongey white pads. On the inside of the clear lid were various diodes and scanners and sensors. Intravenous needles on long tubes could be unhooked and unspooled from inner compartments. The contraption made a quiet, peaceful humming sound that pulsed in and out of earshot.

It was some kind of hyper-advanced medical unit, far beyond the technological capabilities made public by the United Earth Collective. The founders must have spent the fortunes of multiple dynasties getting hold of it.

"What happened to 'human made, humans saved', huh?" Holly wondered aloud. "I guess some humans need saving more than others..."

She spun around as footsteps clomped down the corridor.

"Fritz? Oh, thank God you're back, did you—"

She regretted the words almost as soon as she spoke them.

First, a quartet of gnarly fingers curled around the metal doorframe like the pale roots of a withered tree. They were followed by the waxy, scratched-up face of one of the men who'd come bursting out of the atrium's security office. He grinned like a hyena that's chased its exhausted prey into a dead-end ravine.

"Found you," he rasped triumphantly.

White panic washed over Holly. She staggered backwards against the incubator booth. Her trembling hands alternated between warding off the intruder and rummaging behind her for anything she could use as a weapon. The medical unit was silky smooth to the touch. Her fingers traced a power cable and some kind of on-off button, but nothing else.

The man darted forward. He only covered a couple of feet, and the laugh he barked out indicated he only intended to frighten her, but she lunged towards the opposite side of the operating table all the same. She sprinted to one end; he followed. Back towards the medical unit she went; the man mirrored her movements. He had her trapped.

"You don't belong here," he growled, grabbing the edge of the operating table.

"Then let me fucking leave!"

She feigned left, darted right. Her attacker fell for it, but not for long. By the time she was halfway around the table, he was back where he started, blocking the way out. She tried to turn around but her shoes slipped against the tiles. The man grabbed her from behind and slammed her against the metal table. She felt a blast of pain from somewhere near her kidneys, and the next thing she knew she was face down on the cold, damp floor.

Rough hands pulled Holly over before she could even shake clear the stars from her vision. She blinked open her eyes and screamed.

The face inches from her own was mottled with thin lines of blue and patches of grey. Nothing resided behind the bulging, brown, bloodshot eyes. *Nothing*. It was as if they'd been painted on with a mirror glaze. He stared not at her, but *through* her, as if fascinated by something unseen behind her head. The insane grin remained permanently plastered to his face, the corners twitching with the strain of holding it upright. His fetid breath made her stomach lurch.

Her scream was cut short as his hands wrapped around her throat.

He kept grinning, kept laughing as he choked the life from her. She tried to kick upwards, buried a knee in the man's groin, but he didn't seem to feel a thing. Swinging her fists into his ribcage was no more successful at pushing him off her. She tried choking him in return but, pinned against the floor, gravity wasn't on her side. When her hands climbed the man's pallid face in the hope to scratch his cheeks and gouge his eyes, he simply arched his back further away from her.

"Get... off... me..."

The words, screamed loud inside Holly's head, came out of her mouth as barely a whisper. Each punch she delivered carried less force than the last. Her left arm was in agony – either the wound had reopened in the attack, or the strain of fighting back had torn something new. Fireworks went off inside her skull as oxygen got cut off from her brain.

He was stronger than her. He was unhinged. In a straight brawl, he was unquestionably going to win.

She turned her head as best she could with the man's hands still wrapped around her neck. After being thrown into the operating table, she hadn't been the only thing to fall over. The wheeled tray lay on its side, its surgical tools scattered over the tiles.

With one hand still pushing up against the man's chest, trying desperately to give her throat even a modicum of relief, she stretched the other out and tried to grab one of the fallen instruments. Everything was just out of reach. The largest of the scalpels had rolled towards the small drain in the centre of the room, and the tweezers were closer to the gown and glove bins.

Her vision began to go black. She violently waved her hand back and forth over the tiles, praying for anything. Her fingertips brushed something cold and metal. For a second she thought it was just the nearest wheel of the operating table, but then her skin caught a sharp edge.

Spittle hung from the man's deranged grin. Sweat dripped from the lank strands of hair hanging over his sickly forehead. Something in Holly's throat made a hollow *click* noise as the pressure on it increased.

She stretched as far as she could, unable to turn her head any further to see what it was she'd found. She felt the metal tip of the instrument spin slightly at her touch. A shiver of panic ran through her. Had her shaking fingers pushed it away? But then they found it again, and hungrily pulled it towards her, millimetre by precarious millimetre.

Her chest tightened... Her temples were on fire...

Holly grabbed her weapon and swung it upwards.

Blood spurted across the operating room tiles. Holly felt warmth spread across her chest, but her vision was still too greyed out for her to see why. More importantly, the crushing pressure on her larynx suddenly disappeared. She sucked in air in great, gasping croaks.

Her sight quickly went from a pinprick of light in the distance to a washed out blur. Her croaks became a wheeze, became a scream.

The man kneeling on top of her had a pair of suture scissors impaled through his right eye socket.

Holly scuttled backwards, no longer trapped under his weight, oblivious to the surge of pain once again coursing through her arm, until her back smacked against the cabinets beside the sink. The man remained on his knees where they'd fought, swaying slightly, his hands limp by his sides, the grin twitching harder than ever as it struggled to keep its mad composure. Blood gushed from the wound and ran towards the drain in a great claret river.

Then, with one last hiccup of unsure laughter, he collapsed forwards. The scissors were driven deeper into the man's skull with a nauseating *crunch*.

Holly stared at him – for how long, she couldn't say – terrified that he'd get back up. The man had seemed possessed by something, whether illness or something else altogether. She had to raise her hands up to her face before she realised they were covered in the same sticky blood that continued to seep towards Saturnalia's sewage system.

The faucet of the sink above her head was dripping. She hadn't noticed its rhythmic tapping sound until now. Slowly, almost sedately, her mind began to drift back to that dark plane of disassociation...

She shrieked as a pair of hands grabbed her shoulders.

"It's me," Fritz hissed. "It's just me. My God, Holly. Are you... No, of course you're not okay."

"He..." Her eyes kept flittering between Fritz and the corpse in front of her. "I thought he was... I didn't want to..."

"I know. Shit, I'm sorry. I shouldn't have left you alone."

She felt Fritz pull her up onto her feet. Nothing but a rubber doll, she had to grab hold of the edge of the sink to keep from crashing back to the floor. Suddenly, her stomach pitched. She turned around and threw up half-digested sausage balls into the basin.

"It's okay. He can't hurt you, not anymore." Fritz pulled her towards the door. "But we've gotta go. You know the others will come looking for him."

She wiped her mouth free of vomit with the back of her hand as Fritz dragged her down the corridor towards the access tunnel he'd found. She couldn't tear her eyes from the corpse, and visions of it, clear as a fresh photograph, followed her long after they lost sight of the operating room.

Even if they escaped Saturnalia, nothing for Holly would ever be the same.

CHAPTER
SIXTEEN

The hidden door in the ground floor corridor of the Residential Suites cracked open. One of Fritz's eyes appeared in the gap. As confident as he could be that they were alone, he hurriedly pulled Holly through with him.

She hadn't stopped shaking since the attack in the operating room.

It seemed likely that the same architects who designed the atrium also worked on the suites, for all the walls were panelled in similar oak and trimmed with polished brass. No reflective marble here, though – everything was covered in a fluffy red carpet. Under better circumstances, Holly would have probably slipped her shoes off and scrunched the thick fibres between her bare toes.

Paintings hung in chunky gold frames that must have carried price tags even heftier than the art itself. That said, she vaguely recognised a few as Rembrandts and Monets, plus a Japanese print that she could have sworn was a wallpaper option on her data pad. A stone bust stood on a plinth in the corner, flanked by two potted plants with fat, green leaves.

"Which way?" Holly asked. She needed a drink; her words cracked like mud under a hot sun.

"Couldn't tell you," Fritz replied distractedly. He approached the nearest corner and checked both ways down the corridor. "The main elevator should take us up to the Resort, I think. Let's try this way."

"And you're sure you don't remember where the maids' service corridors are?"

"We wouldn't be out here if I did."

He went to progress down the corridor, but Holly remained motionless. Well, almost motionless. She was still shaking like crazy.

"Just one second," she said, before staggering back in the opposite direction.

"What—" Fritz shook his head as he followed. "Where the hell are you going?"

"I don't... It won't take a second."

Holly knew that the main entrance of the suites had to be back this way because the pharmacy building ran parallel to it. Her head was woozy, her body felt like it was one misstep away from falling to pieces, but she wasn't stupid. They'd been walking around at right angles. She knew if she kept heading in this direction, she would eventually hit the fancy glass-and-gold doors they saw behind the barricaded iron gate outside.

And she was right. The lobby was just past their corridor. A smaller version of the atrium, it was split into two levels – a lower section with visitor seating and wall-mounted postal boxes, and, a few steps above that, an upper tier dominated by its concierge desk. The touch-screen computer hidden behind the counter reflected the dazzling crystals of the chandelier above. The doors were barricaded on the inside, too – a plush sofa had been dragged away from its spot beside an abstract-looking coffee table to keep them from swinging inwards. A long trail of blood stretched across the marble floor from the entrance to a corridor on the other side.

"Jesus, Holly." Fritz caught up with her. "What are you doing, wandering about like this? You're lucky there isn't anyone else here."

"That's not true," Holly said with zero emotion. "He is."

She pointed to a body slumped against the wall beside the reception desk. The man wore a black footman's top hat and tails. One of his shoes had fallen off, and Holly felt a bizarre compulsion to slip it back over his sock.

"Yes, well, he should be all the warning we need not to hang around here any longer than we have to." Fritz tugged at Holly's arm. "I might not know the precise layout of the upper sectors, but I *do* know the elevators are located near the back."

"One second." She pulled away from him. "There's something I need to check first."

Worried that Holly's mind had been fractured beyond repair, Fritz kept close behind.

There was no real need for post boxes on Saturnalia, because there was no real post. Nobody sent each other letters anymore, and any digital messages to friends, family or business partners were delivered off-station by the now-defunct comms array. But if Holly had learned nothing else about the station since her arrival, it was that appearances were more important than common sense. As such, there were slots for all eighty-something apartments. From a quick glance into those whose doors had been busted open, some were used as temporary lockboxes, others as a way for workers and respected employees like Dr. Humphreys to deliver goods and necessities to the residents without ever needing to interact with them directly.

Holly cared about none of this. All she was looking for was a name and apartment number.

"Walton, Al Saud, Caan... come on... Aha! *L. & R. Flynn*, number 513."

"Not this again. There isn't time, Holly. You said it yourself, we need to get a message out to the company before everyone here suffocates to death."

"And what was it you said, back in the Workers' District when you wanted to check your own quarters? Ah, yes. *It's on the way.* It's not like we're going door to door. We'll be in and out in no time."

"Aren't you overlooking something rather important?"

"What?"

"If the door to apartment 513 is locked, how do you plan to get inside?"

"I'll knock. If Mrs. Flynn is still alive, she can let us in."

"Will she? Would *you?* Even if she's expecting somebody to come rescue her, how will she know you're telling the truth?"

Holly made a loud huffing noise, then stomped around to the back of the concierge desk. The touch-screen monitor was completely intact and operational, but when she woke it with a brush of her finger she was faced with a password login. She typed in PASSWORD, then SATURNALIA. Neither worked. She let out a grunt of frustration.

"Hey, won't you take a break for a second?" Fritz chased after her. "You were almost killed back there. I know I said we were in a hurry and all, but, well, maybe we could both use a bit of a sit down..."

"Oh, no, can't do that." Holly started pulling open cabinet drawers at random. "No, we're in *much* too big a rush, Fritz."

"Holly..."

She triumphantly brandished a brass device shaped like a triangular utility key.

"Master key. I knew they'd have one somewhere. Imagine if there was a station-wide blackout and everyone got stuck inside their rooms. Always need an old-fashioned manual override."

She stormed off down the corridor again, more steady on her feet than before. Fritz threw his hands in the air and tried to keep pace.

"Slow down a moment, won't you? What's gotten into you? I think you're in shock. *Mein Gott.* I wish Dr. Humphreys wasn't dead..."

"The doctor is dead?"

"Hmm? Oh, yes. Found him upstairs. Sorry, with the state you were in, I forgot—"

"It's okay. It's not like we expected to find many survivors anyway, right?"

Fritz bowed his head and said nothing. Holly felt a mild twang of guilt – the first proper emotion she'd felt since the attack. She should have bit her tongue. Maria was still out there somewhere, either dead or alive. More likely the former.

They turned right at the end of the corridor, past the hidden door back to the pharmacy (it had since clicked shut, and was indistinguishable from the other sections of oak-panelled wall) and the stone bust with its two flanking houseplants. The next corridor was about the same length and ended in another right turn. Holly suspected that if she followed it to its eventual conclusion, she'd end up right back in the lobby again.

A set of elevator doors stood in a sunken enclave to their right. Holly quickened her pace further. She was close. She could feel it. Her heart quivered and she found it difficult to swallow, and not just because of the bruising around her neck.

Directly opposite the elevator was Michelangelo's David. It was an impressive replica. They'd even managed to capture the cracks on the leg and toes.

"Huh. Look at that," she said, glancing back at it over her shoulder as she pushed the button to call the elevator. "Almost looks like it could be the original."

"Does it?" Fritz gave the statue a gentle flick with his finger. "Wouldn't know. Never seen it before."

Holly kept prodding the elevator call button. Nothing was happening.

"Goddammit. Elevator's out. Please tell me the people living here weren't afraid of climbing a few stairs."

Fritz backtracked to an unmarked door with a slender inset window. He tried the handle; it was unlocked. He cracked it open and nodded.

"In here," he said anxiously. "Not much room to run if any residents find us, though."

"Better than if they caught us inside the elevator," Holly replied, pushing past him through the door. He sighed and obediently followed.

If she'd expected a bland, concrete stairwell like that of the Flynn Industries offices back on New Terra, she'd be wrong. Brass bannister railings followed the inside of the stairs. The outside walls were covered with interlocking bamboo shoots, stained dark. Despite the splendour, the patterned carpet wasn't in the slightest bit faded. Holly wondered whether it had sampled so much as a single stiletto heel since Saturnalia first opened its doors to residents.

The doughy carpet softened their footsteps. Holly couldn't help taking the steps more quickly than she probably should have given the consequences of being heard or spotted. The higher they climbed, the closer she got to fulfilling her reason for coming to Saturnalia in the first place.

First floor, second floor, third...

After all this time, to get this near—

A loud bang reverberated down the stairwell. Holly froze; Fritz almost tipped over backwards with the suddenness of his stop and had to grab hold of the brass railing for balance. It sounded like a door being slammed open a couple of floors above. They paused, motionless, barely even a glance shared between them. But then they heard a second knock and realised it was just Saturnalia's pipes experiencing yet another bout of indigestion. They continued their ascent, albeit more cautiously than before, casting a suspicious eye over the door of each landing they passed.

They arrived at the fifth floor. Already depleted of energy to begin with, now Holly felt like even the bones in her legs were starting to chip away. The stairs rose no further and only one door awaited them. With the master key clasped in one hand, Holly inched opened the door with her other.

Deserted. Or at least the corridor was – already she could see multiple apartment doors, some shut, others smashed off their hinges. Any number of bloodthirsty killers could be stalking through the complex's various rooms. This was their home, after all.

513. She needed to find apartment 513.

She slipped out, held the door open for Fritz. He shut it behind them slowly enough for its catch not to make a sound. Shattered glass lay on the carpet close to the doorway from where a lamp had been smashed. They carefully stepped around it. An astronomically large television inside one of the rooms whose door was open spat out an endless monologue of sharp static. The white snowstorm of its screen conjured long unnerving shadows across the rest of the dark apartment.

They gave this a wide berth, too.

502. 501. They were headed backwards, but that was fine – if it was anything like the lobby down on the ground floor, the corridor would loop back on itself anyway. 516. Holly's heart leapt. 515. It had to be around here somewhere...

She stopped beside the door marked 513. Her heart lost its grip on the lofty mountain face of her throat and plummeted to its doom in the pit of her stomach. In her disappointment, she let the master key slip from her fingers.

The door was thrown wide open. The apartment inside was in ruin.

"Still want to go in?" Fritz whispered, bending down to pick up the discarded key.

By way of an answer, she crept across the threshold.

The Flynn couple's apartment put museums to shame. Holly had never seen so many display plinths and glass cabinets before in her life – and this was just the entrance hall. She spotted African tribal masks hanging inside one broken case, a Stradivarius violin that somebody had snapped in half, and almost swore in surprise when she came face to face with a Tyrannosaurus rex skull rescued from the Natural History Museum. It was still intact despite the vandalism elsewhere, thankfully, though one of the intruders appeared to have wrapped one of Mr. Flynn's ties around its tooth.

She tiptoed between the exhibits, her eyes flitting from corner to corner as she scoured the apartment for survivors, friendly or otherwise. The huge, mounted head of a tusked boar watched her – and then a resistant Fritz, unwilling to linger out in the corridor by himself – pass under the vast archway onto which it and numerous other unfortunate creatures were nailed.

They entered the living room. Again, the sheer scale of the place was overwhelming. A dozen of the quarters in the Worker District's could have fit inside – and the Flynns were barely even *using* any of it! A colossal C-shaped sofa curved towards an artificial fireplace and a wall of ultra-high definition panels (now broken) capable of summoning an assortment of digital landscapes. A snow-swept mountaintop scene glitched on and off. A grand piano occupied the corner opposite, its keys smashed and strings cut. Aside from a few vases and the obligatory chandelier hanging overhead, most of the hall consisted or pure empty space.

Holly supposed that when you were the sole heir of an industrialist whose net worth overshadowed many countries' GDPs, the best way to demonstrate your wealth was to prove you could acquire real-estate for the sole purpose of doing nothing with it.

The smell of orange and camomile was overwhelmed by a sudden coppery odour. Holly looked down as her shoe struggled to unglue itself from a puddle of dark stickiness. Raising her head, she noticed a pair of legs ending in smart black pumps sticking out from behind the protracted sofa.

"Oh God," she gasped, too numb to shriek despite the plunging dread that overcame her. "Please don't be Rosie, please don't—"

It was another of the housemaids. She'd been slaughtered while she worked. Somebody had slit her belly open with a cleaver before jamming part of a modern art sculpture into her mouth. Well, Holly hoped it had been before, at any rate. Teeth were everywhere except where they should be.

"It isn't Maria." Fritz sagged against the sofa in relief and broke into a miserable, hysterical smile. "I was certain it was her for a moment. *Gott*. I think I might throw up. It's one thing to feel something is true, and another to see it with your own two eyes, you know?"

But Holly wasn't listening to him. If the killers had gotten into Mrs. Flynn's apartment while the housemaids were still working, then who was to say the same fate hadn't awaited the suite's occupants, too?

"Rosie?" She sprinted into the adjoining master bedroom. "Rosie, it's me, Holly. Please answer me. Are you in here?"

The bed had a larger square footage than the shuttle that brought her to Saturnalia. Its covers and sheets were in disarray, and all the cupboards and drawers had been pulled open and the pretty dresses and pressed shirts within strewn over the floor. Clearly Holly wasn't the first person to come looking for the Flynns. She crossed the room and checked the expansive en suite. Nobody hiding in there, either. She spun around looking everywhere, unsure what to do next.

It was time to face reality. Suite 513 was empty.

Holly collapsed onto the edge of the bed, buried her head in her hands and burst into tears.

"Fuck. I thought she'd be here. I really did."

"Hey, are you all right?" Fritz approached gingerly. He went to pat her on the shoulder but thought better of it. "It's okay. Really. You did all you could, but you don't owe the

Flynns anything. It's just a job. What matters is keeping yourself alive, right?"

"No, you don't understand. I didn't…"

Holly visibly deflated. She shook her head. There was no use in hiding the truth any longer.

"Rosie Flynn isn't my employer, Fritz. She's my sister."

CHAPTER
SEVENTEEN

Holly fished out the photograph from her back pocket. The corners were crumpled and the creases bone-white. She handed it to Fritz.

"I'm the kid," she explained. "My sister, Rosie, is the one crawling across the floor. Trying to get away from us," she added with a spiteful raise of her eyebrow.

"And these two, they're your parents?" Fritz asked, stating the obvious.

"Yeah. Michael and Sasha Bloom. Mum and Dad. They were lucky enough to win tickets aboard the Arks back when they first ran the lottery. They weren't considered essential workers – they never would have got off-world otherwise. They were real young, too. So when they had me later in life, they were surprised. Must have been knocked for six when my sister popped out a few years later."

"Ah." Fritz plopped down on the bed beside her. "I think I can see where this is going."

"Yeah. Two tickets, four family members. The number you were allocated was all you got – certainly if you got them for free. Otherwise people would have crammed their parents and grandparents and second-cousins into their cabins with them. So Mum and Dad arranged for the tickets to be put under my name and Rosie's name instead. When the Arks finally took off from Earth in 2072, my parents stayed behind."

Fritz nodded.

"I was an only child, and my parents had passed long before the Arks left. But Maria had to leave behind her brother and her elderly mother. It broke her heart."

"Exodus was nine years ago, so I was, what? Twenty-one when we left Earth? Yeah, that sounds about right. And Rosie was just seventeen. We were old enough to understand why our parents couldn't come with us. That was a small blessing, at least. Unfortunately, we weren't quite old enough to be left alone to fend for ourselves on a spaceship hurtling through time and space. We weren't irresponsible," she suddenly added, as if she'd somehow incriminated herself. "Just terrified, that's all."

"Hey. That trip scared the shit out of me, too."

Holly took the photograph back, cradled it in her lap.

"Rosie and I stuck together for most of the time we were in orbit above New Terra. I'd already graduated from school, but there wasn't much in the way of work on the Ark for someone like me to do, so that's when I signed up for analyst training. There was a list of in-demand professions, and I've always been good with numbers, so..." Holly shrugged. "Rosie still had to balance her education with work experience until we got planet-side, so she took a job waiting tables at Maynard & Brown's – some fancy steak joint over in the Platinum Sector where everyone who bought their Ark tickets lived. There were easier assignments, by far. I think she just wanted to see how the other half lived."

Holly gestured to the purple and velveted opulence around them.

"Well, she got a damn good look, didn't she? Because that's where she met... *him*."

"Mr. Flynn? Lucky lady."

"Yeah, I guess that's one way of looking at it. Lewis Flynn was – *is* – an entitled arsehole who never saw something pretty he couldn't get his hands on. Spent all his time on the Ark getting drunk in the Spacebar, waiting for this place to become operational. He kept inviting Rosie to join him – you know, outside of her working hours. At first I egged her on – like you said, lucky lady, right? – but then the two of us started to drift apart. She was standoffish whenever I brought up the age gap between them. She'd not come back to our dorm for days, sometimes a week at a time. Eventually she stopped talking to me at all."

"I know it's none of my business," Fritz said gently, his eyes darting to the living room, "and I don't know the full story, but could it be you misjudged the guy? I'm not saying he isn't an arsehole," he hurriedly added, "but they did end up hitched, after all."

"Maybe." Holly sighed. "It's not like she ever tried to introduce me to him, or anything. I might have assumed he was a piece of shit just because he belonged to a different class, that it was for that reason alone Rosie and I grew apart. But I don't think so. Rosie was an impressionable young thing. I think Lewis Flynn had her wrapped around his finger the second he laid eyes on her.

"When the announcement came that said everyone was to head down to New Terra and complete the colonisation process, I was so excited. Finally, we could breathe real air on a real planet, sleep in homes instead of coffin bunks, find jobs and build a new life for ourselves. A fresh start for everyone. I immediately called Rosie to ask if she'd heard the news – and this time, to my surprise, she actually answered. But she told me she wasn't coming. Lewis had offered to take her with him to Saturnalia, and she'd accepted. I'm not an idiot. I knew that we wouldn't live together as sisters forever. But I thought we'd at least share the same fucking planet."

Fritz had risen from the bed and was now anxiously checking the way back out of the apartment.

"Yeah," he said, making a valiant but unconvincing effort to not sound as distracted as he looked. "To survive the evacuation of Earth together, only to lose her over some guy – that's one hell of a kick in the teeth."

Holly felt like scrunching the photograph up into a ball and throwing it across the bedroom. Photo paper was expensive, but she had the original saved on a data drive back home and a copy backed up on the extranet. Instead she leaned forwards and slipped it back into her rear pocket.

"So I got shuttled down to New Terra while Rosie stayed on the Ark. It was only a few years later when I read a report on the grand opening of Saturnalia that I saw the two of them had got married. She hadn't spoken to me in all that time, not even to tell me they were engaged. Still hasn't spoken to me."

"Wait. So Rosie Flynn *didn't* ask you to come rescue her?"

"No. I lied. Sorry. I had no idea any of this was going to happen, and I can't imagine she did, either. I was just so lonely, and so worried. I'd lost everyone. So I got a job at Flynn Industries as an analyst and bided my time until I could volunteer to come out here. I thought I could either check that Rosie truly was okay without me, that she wasn't trapped here like another trophy in the Flynn family collection, or convince her to come back home. To her real family, I mean. Me."

"Shit, Holly. No wonder you were so keen to find Mrs. Flynn before getting off this station. I'm... well, I'm sorry. I wouldn't have pushed back the way I did if I'd known."

"Yeah, well." Holly rose from the bed, sniffed, and wiped the drying tears from her cheek with her finger. "I left it too late, didn't I? If my sister wasn't in a bad way before, she sure as hell is now."

"Hey, you don't know that. You haven't found a body. For all you know, she's still out there somewhere, trying to figure a way off this station just like us."

Holly smiled sorrowfully.

"Like Maria?"

"Yeah... Yeah, like Maria, I guess. So how about we get moving and see if we can't find them?"

She nodded and went to leave, but a small, black flyer on the nightstand caught her eye. She picked it up and gave it a once over.

"Hey, Fritz. When did you say all this madness started?"

"Erm, it was three days ago, I think. So... April the twenty-third? Hard to be sure. Why'd you ask?"

She looked back down at the flyer. A blonde sexagenarian in a sequinned dress and feather boa was bellowing into a microphone whilst fighting off the glare of a blinding spotlight. *Madame Gosselin*, it read. *Matinee and evening performances available*. The same date was printed across the bottom in silver cursive. *April 23rd*.

"No reason," she replied, letting the flyer fall to the messy floor. "All this violence had to start somewhere. I was just wondering who – or what – first set it off."

CHAPTER
EIGHTEEN

They lingered inside the front door of apartment 513 as footsteps thundered down the corridor outside. Holly held onto the handle with her foot wedged against the door while Fritz had his back to the wall and a broken table leg raised over his shoulder like a club.

For the first time since Fritz snatched Holly to keep her from falling prey to the prowling psychopaths in Engineering, they felt like a team rather than two forces pulling in opposing directions.

Whoever was sprinting through the suites disappeared around the corner. They waited for a few seconds before widening the gap to check that the coast was clear.

"Okay," Fritz said, his head swerving from side to side like a weathervane. "Let's go."

"Keep an eye on the doors," Holly hissed urgently. "More of them could come from anywhere."

They continued following the corridor round to the left. Fritz stuck close to the wall as if it might provide even a shred of cover should a less-than-amicable resident wander out of a neighbouring suite. Holly followed in a hurried tiptoe, ready to sprint like a startled gazelle.

Conversation, and Holly didn't think it came from a TV. They ducked into the closest open doorway together, hoping the room wasn't occupied. The apartment was smaller than Rosie's, which made its ransacking appear much worse; it probably only belonged to a billionaire of the nine-figure variety – how embarrassing for them. The lights were smashed out and a painting of Guru Nanak, the founder of Sikhism, had been cut violently from its frame. The door had been broken – its lock and hinges were loose, and the wood had been splintered and buckled inwards along its middle – but they could creak it far enough shut to hide behind.

Somebody emerged from the apartment beside theirs, laughed to themself in its doorway, then strolled merrily by.

"Whereas I was blind," the unseen man sang as he passed their door, "now I see…"

The lunatic whistled shrilly as he scraped a pool cue down the length of the corridor wall.

"There are no—"

He turned the corner with a skip in his step and his child-like lyrics became indecipherable. Holly gawped at Fritz.

"Still think it was a class uprising? Monocle or no monocle, that man was an utter fruitcake."

"No, I… I think something else has afflicted rich and poor alike. Something worse." Fritz nervously pulled open the door. "We should get upstairs as soon as we can."

Holly quickly pushed it closed again.

"And how are we even supposed to get to the Resort District, anyway?" she whispered. "The elevator was out of order, remember?"

"Different elevator," he replied. "Runs off a separate generator in Engineering, too. I should know – I've serviced it enough times. It still might not be operational, of course."

"What will we do if it isn't?"

"Find some stairs, I guess?" Fritz gave a quick, nervous shrug. "The maintenance elevator also shipped workers up to the Resort floor, but obviously that's out of commission as well. There must be some service tunnels between here and there, though."

"But you don't know where they are?"

"Nope. Through another of those secret doors, I imagine."

"Those secret doors that are imperceptible to the naked eye?"

Fritz gave her a deadpan stare.

"The ones indistinguishable from the wall panels, yes."

"Perfect." Holly let him open the door again. "There's no way we're getting murdered in here."

They followed the corridor further around, away from the singing resident. Hopefully he didn't plan on patrolling the whole way around. Some of the other doors they passed were still locked, as if the occupants had not done anything to incur the wrath delivered elsewhere. Did they belong to the killers? Holly shuddered at the thought of somebody spying on them from the other side of their peepholes.

"There." Fritz turned and shook her by the shoulder. "The Resort elevator, do you see it?"

It was hard not to. Now Holly understood why the elevators were kept separate. Heading up to the Resort District was clearly meant to be a Big Deal for everyone involved. Above the round, spacious cabin was a curved sign reading PARADISE AWAITS. The words were outlined with small, flashing bulbs like those you'd expect to find attached to signs advertising shows on London's West End. Rotund and gilded, the elevator cabin looked like a Ferris Wheel carriage that had been designed by Jules Verne.

Following a quick risk analysis of the adjacent corridor, they scurried across to the elevator's small, pillared alcove. The doors of the cabin were already open. A curved, cushioned bench ran around the rest of its interior, and Holly felt a strong compulsion to sit on it. It wasn't as if they had anywhere to run. They'd willingly trapped themselves. *Again.*

Fritz studied the operating panel. As with the rickety, old elevator behind Father O'Brien's church, there was only the one button for both Up and Down. They both brightened as it made a jovial *buh-ling* sound upon him pressing it.

The doors didn't close.

"Let me try," Holly said, jabbing her thumb against the button. The same *buh-ling* noise; the same inanimate doors. "Oh, come *on*..."

"Maybe a mechanical error?" Fritz suggested. "Or wiring, perhaps – if I had more time I could—"

Faint whistling stopped their hushed conversation short. The merry resident was making a return trip. They looked at one another in mortified panic.

"You don't have more time," Holly hissed. "Fix it now!"

Fritz tried to pry the panel free, but it was bolted onto the elevator's frame. Fingers and brute strength wouldn't cut it. He needed his tool kit – the whole point of the damn thing was to be as hard as possible for unqualified people to open. He checked the rest of the cabin, but – aside from an emergency call button, and he sure as hell wasn't pressing *that* – their only option was the lone button for going up.

He jabbed it again.

Buh-ling.

The doors stayed put. The whistling got louder.

Buh-ling!

Still nothing.

"Why don't you press it again?" Holly teetered on the verge of hysterics. "I don't think we've tried that yet!"

"I don't see *you* doing much, Holly!"

They both stiffened as the whistling resident ambled down the corridor beside the elevator, spinning his pool cue around like a rifleman on parade. He stopped directly in front of the cabin and, with a toothy grin, turned to look at them both with a total lack of surprise, as if they'd arranged to meet there.

"Why, hello there, friends," he crooned. "I don't think *you're* supposed to be here."

Holly reached across Fritz and hammered the button as hard and as rapidly as she could. The man dropped his cue and sprinted towards the cabin, honking like a sea lion. Fritz shrank back to the far wall and crashed onto the bench.

Buh-ling.

The doors suddenly rumbled along their tracks and slammed shut just as the madman reached them. He didn't seem particularly angry at the setback. Still laughing his weird honking laugh, he slammed his palms against the other side of the doors like a child trying to rile up monkeys at the zoo.

The elevator trundled upwards. The banging grew quieter. Holly collapsed onto the bench beside Fritz and let out a staggered whimper.

"I'm starting to think we should have just barricaded ourselves inside the Workers' Canteen," she sighed.

"Then we'd suffocate or freeze to death along with everyone else."

"I fail to see how that wouldn't be preferable."

The elevator stopped with a sickening lurch. Its cabin was plunged into darkness. The steady background chugging noise whirred off into silence.

"Shit. Do you think that guy cut the power?"

Fritz shook his head and tried pressing the button again. No jovial *buh-ling* noise this time. At least the elevator didn't rattle back down the way it came.

"No, I don't think so. Not that quickly."

An ear-splitting wail overwhelmed the station. Holly covered her ears. The world around her went from silvery-midnight to blood red.

"See?" Fritz shouted over the noise. "That's the alarm. Power failure. Remember what I told you? Saturnalia's systems are shutting down."

"Can you get this thing started again?"

"Not a chance. The elevator's fine – it's the corresponding generator that's the problem. This isn't moving until we fix that."

"No way am I going all the way back down to Engineering. So, what? We're stuck in here?"

Fritz stepped up onto the bench and gave the ceiling a hesitant punch. The panel in the centre of the cabin roof came free.

"Not necessarily."

Despite Holly's confused protestations, Fritz clambered up through the resulting hole and disappeared into the darkness above. She stood alone for a moment that felt like a minute, her arms flapping by her sides in anticipation, before his hand reappeared and offered to help pull her up.

She stared at it in spluttering bemusement, shrugged, and finally grabbed his hand. Luckily, Fritz was stronger than his wiry frame had her believe. She assured herself she could have climbed up alone had it not been for her manky arm, but that probably wasn't true.

The emergency lights were even redder outside the cabin, and the wailing siren all the more shrill. Once on the flat roof of the otherwise round elevator, she nervously rose to her feet – the metal groaned and creaked and buckled slightly under weight.

"Mother of…" She struggled to maintain her balance. "Is this safe, Fritz?"

"I won't lie to you," he replied, retaking her hand while holding onto one of the elevator cables for support. "Do you see those doors up there?"

To Holly, most of the elevator shaft resembled nothing but steel girders, sheets, and bolts holding the sheets and girders together. But about a dozen metres further up, close to the end of the vertical tunnel, was a section of wall that looked split down the middle. A ladder ran the length of the shaft; the last few rungs stopped beside it.

"Yeah, just about. Is that the Resort District?"

"That's the only other stop this elevator goes to, so yeah."

"And you can open them?"

"Definitely. There's always a manual release from inside the shaft. It's regulation, even here."

"Best news I've heard all day."

"Now," Fritz said, gently releasing Holly's hand and stretching for the wall beside the elevator cabin, "we just need to make our way up there."

Holly staggered for a moment, untethered, before grabbing hold of the same cable as Fritz. It was oily and sticky. She hated going near it. If the elevator suddenly fell, either she'd be left hanging above a deadly drop or the friction from the cable would burn her hand off.

With only his fingertips still touching the cable, Fritz

took hold of the closest rung on the wall. He gave another rung at his feet a good kick before deciding it was safe to use. He let go of the cable and put his full weight on the ladder.

"Seems safe," he whispered back to her. "Hope you're not scared of heights."

"Not scared," Holly sighed, shaking as she went to follow. "Terrified."

Resisting the urge to look down through the gap between the elevator cabin and the wall, Holly crossed to the ladder as quickly as her trembling legs allowed. Her hands were slick with sweat. She wiped each of them in turn against her shirt before climbing after Fritz – he was already a good few metres ahead of her.

She wished the alarm would stop screaming. The ominous red murder-lights she could deal with, but if Saturnalia's demise was imminent, she didn't need to greet it with perforated ear drums.

She thought her legs had recovered from their climb up the stairwell, but they soon returned to stone. Each step to the next rung required gargantuan effort. And no matter how hard Holly pushed herself, Fritz's lead on her kept on growing.

Until it didn't.

"Here," he said, his quiet voice ricocheting down the elevator shaft from the top of the ladder. "Shouldn't even take a minute."

"Wait," she gasped. "Hold up a second..."

There was a light *clang* as Fritz swung open the lid of the case housing the manual release. Holly had no idea what that manual release entailed – was it a complicated nest of cables and switches he needed to hot wire, or was there simply a lever to be pulled down like a fire alarm? She presumed the latter – emergency exits were usually kept as simple as possible, for obvious reasons. Then again, untrained locals weren't expected to go climbing around inside the shaft, either. She gritted her teeth and fought against the concrete inside her thighs as she struggled to hurry after him.

A leaden *thunk* rang out as the locks securing the Resort District doors disengaged. Holly glanced up and gulped as Fritz stretched across the divide between ladder and doorway in order to pry the two halves apart. Neither the rung nor the sill jutting out from the elevator doorway gave him more than a few inches of foot room.

Fishing his fingers into the gap between the doors and using the ladder as an anchor, Fritz heaved against the door closest to him. At first it didn't give, and Holly wondered if maybe the power cut hadn't also put the sector on lockdown, but then it suddenly rolled across its tracks with so little resistance Fritz almost swung off the ladder completely. Connected to it by just a single hand and foot, Fritz flailed until he could wrap his hand around the inside of the door and clumsily pull himself through the resulting square of bright light.

Holly still had half a dozen metres to climb when Fritz's silhouette disappeared. She took the ladder one rung at a time, the muscles in her arms aching as bad as her legs now, their weakness threatening to cast her back down into the iron gloom below. Finally, so exhausted she couldn't see straight, she drew close enough for the blinding glare to clear and for the shapes of the Resort District to begin to take form...

...and the door slowly rolled to a close again.

"Fritz? *Fritz?*" She scrambled upwards, dead legs be damned. "You have got to be... Get back here, you bloody idiot!"

A foot darted into the gap to keep the doors from locking shut, and then a calloused hand pried them open again.

"Keep your voice down," Fritz hissed. "I'm not going anywhere."

He took her hand. Following an ill-judged peek back down the ladder, half-expecting the madman to be climbing up after them with the pool cue clenched between his teeth, Holly allowed Fritz to swiftly pull her across the empty expanse – albeit with her eyes shut and her bladder ready to empty itself. Once she was safely through, he removed his foot again, and the doors lethargically locked shut behind them.

She collapsed against the nearest potted succulent, took in her first view of the Resort District, and broke into a sardonic smile of incredulity.

"Ah. So *this* is where all the money went."

alf of the slot machines remained operational despite the slow shutdown of Saturnalia. Their speakers bleated out a cacophonous wail of inane electronic ditties while their screens flashed colourfully with endless, oblivious enthusiasm. Holly saw a greater number of digital cherries roll past her eyes in her first few minutes inside the Resort District than she had of the real fruit in her whole lifetime.

A long craps table. A roulette wheel, backed by an enormous display that mirrored the device's spins. Half a dozen poker tables, torn and bent cards cast across their scuffed, verdant surfaces. Tables for pool and snooker, too, most of their cues missing and the coloured balls tossed around the casino floor. Twin bars and accompanying lounge sofas, the bottles smashed from their shelves.

And above it all, a great domed ceiling painted with a curved panorama depicting an elaborate and decadent Roman feast. Fat and wealthy men laughed and drank while nubile girls pranced and danced around them in the nude.

"Earth tore itself apart," Holly mumbled beside the

potted plant outside the elevator doors. "Humanity could barely afford to colonise New Terra even with all its resources combined. And the elite decided to spend their immense wealth on *this?*"

"Here's something that'll really wind you up. There's not even any point to it."

"What do you mean?"

"No actual money changes hands," Fritz explained. "That's what Yassine who works one of the tables told me, anyway. The residents get their allocation of chips from the office, then return their 'winnings' at the end of the evening – if they have any left, that is. Win or lose, it doesn't matter. It's all for show."

"The house always wins," Holly mused, "because they *are* the house."

Fritz shrugged.

"Every aspect of their life here is pre-paid. I don't see what good it would do them to win each other's money, anyway."

A braying laugh burst out of nowhere. Holly flinched and cowered further behind the plastic succulent. But it was only part of a pre-recorded message playing from a nearby popcorn dispenser. The food inside looked stale and slightly burnt.

"How do we get up to the administrator's office?" she asked, already keen to leave.

"From what I understand, the Resort District is directly connected to Operations and Observation by a grand staircase on the far side of this sector. But I've never been through the Resort floor myself."

"The observation deck. Is that the part of the station where you can see Saturn?"

"Yes. Saturnalia's tidally locked, so the gallery is always facing the planet."

Holly let out the quietest whistle she could muster.

"Bet it's a great view. No wonder they keep it within easy reach of the resort-goers. I guess we keep our heads down and look out for signposts, then."

They crept past the one-armed bandits, ignoring the gaudy assault of flashing buttons and virtual board games and trivia readouts as best they could. One had been smashed apart and all the worthless tokens had spilled from the machine's belly in a plastic avalanche. Rosie had always enjoyed playing Dad's retro videogame consoles growing up, and Holly wondered how long her sister had spent inside Saturnalia's casino, gambling with money that didn't exist, trying to recapture the priceless joy of childhood and stave off insanity in this strange, soulless, artificial place.

Another corpse, tucked behind the blackjack tables. Quite a few, in fact – a dozen, perhaps, some in evening wear, others in casino uniform. It seemed as if the killers still lurking Saturnalia's halls had collected their victims into a single heap. Good to keep the place tidy, Holly supposed, before cursing herself for being so blasé. These were real people, slaughtered by their neighbours – possibly their friends.

"Hold on." She grabbed Fritz. "Listen. The alarm's stopped."

"Huh. So it has." Fritz didn't appear as excited by this revelation as she'd hoped. "Somebody in Administration must have switched it off. Maybe Andrew Yang is holed up in there. If he's alive, he could help us."

"If he's alive, do you think he could do more to help save this place than turning off a damn klaxon?"

The Resort District extended far beyond the casino floor.

Past a pair of comically oversized bouquet-bushes of chrysanthemums was a wall of video-posters advertising the other facilities available. A cinema offering select movies from before Earth's collapse; restaurants and bars with an ever-revolving menu of dishes and playlists; a deluxe spa complete with sauna and dedicated pools for relaxation, contemplation and exercise; and a top-of-the-line, multi-user VR room offering interactive experiences of both the old world and the new galaxy – because apparently life on Saturnalia wasn't enough of an escape from reality as it was.

One particular attraction caught Holly's eye so effectively that she stopped halfway across the aisle, completely exposed. She quickly remembered herself and scurried across to the pillar behind which Fritz was hiding.

"Did you see that?" she whispered. "They've got a fucking *beach* here? I've never even *seen* a beach!"

"And you didn't think to pack your swimsuit? *Gott*, I wouldn't be too jealous if I were you. I heard the sand isn't actually real. Mostly."

Holly watched the video-screen as perfectly azure waves lapped against a shore of yellow and gold. The leaves of palm trees swayed in a gentle tropical breeze. An attractive couple with impeccable teeth and a shortage of clothing grinned as they clinked exotic cocktails together.

Prosperity Bay, the overlaid text read. *Let us wash your worries away.*

Worries? Holly scoffed. Christ Almighty. Before this week, what worries did anyone in this place possibly have?

She looked to Fritz, realised with a frosty stab of panic that he wasn't there. Shit. A manic shake of her head revealed his new position, crouched behind a grand, circular, multi-tiered fountain that served as a nexus point for the Resort District. Aisles split off from it towards other sections like the rays of an Aztec sun. She was halfway across to him when he spotted her and gestured for her to hurry over with an alarmed expression on his face.

He pulled her into cover. Past the serene gurgling and trickling of the fountain's various elaborate jets and water-falls, Holly caught the approaching conversation.

"He says the last of 'em are trapped in the Andronicus," a woman with a scratchy British accent shouted to her companion. "Can't be many more of 'em hidden about the station any longer."

"Yeah, but how're we s'posed to get to them?" replied an American man with a southern drawl. "Damn theatre's locked up tighter than Fort Knox. Robinson's been trying to break through for days."

"Didn't have a rescue saw though, did he?" The woman cackled. "Zara brought one up from Engineering. Had to drag it all the way through Hydroponics after what they gone and done to the elevator. Gonna be through that barricade in no time, you'll see."

The voices grew quieter. Holly nudged Fritz.

"Did you hear that? There *are* other survivors on board. Holy crap..." Her eyes widened. "Do you remember that flyer in Rosie's suite? It was for the matinee performance on the day everything went to shit, right? Do you think she might be holed up in this Andronicus place, too?"

Fritz opened and closed his mouth, overwhelmed by her sudden torrent of questions. He shook his head in delibera-tion, then shrugged.

"I guess so? I mean, who's to say she was even going to the show, or if she was, that the staff had opened the doors yet... But sure. She could be, you know? You know her better than me – what do *you* think she'd do?"

Holly sighed.

"I'm not sure I *do* know her better, Fritz. But there's one way to find out."

She rose from the wall of the fountain and crept after the voices. Fritz gawped in frustrated disbelief.

"What are you...? Holly! If the psychopaths can't get inside the theatre, neither can we!"

She paused beside a tall, cascading philodendron.

"There are other survivors, Fritz. Others who haven't lost their minds. Even if Rosie isn't one of them, we have a responsibility to help however we can."

"Cut the hero act," Fritz whispered, chasing after her. "If you didn't think Rosie was alive in there, you'd be running in the opposite direction."

Holly pretended not to hear him, not least because she knew he was right.

The path to the theatre was mercifully brief and not without plenty of gardens and poster boards to hide behind. It was only shortly after leaving the churning waters of the fountain that they heard the mad chatter of locals outside. Holly kept a good distance behind the two conversationalists at all times, never leaving the shadowy cover of the rich, flanking foliage cordoned off by ruby ropes. When she glimpsed the façade of the Andronicus playhouse through the dense foliage, she ventured no further. The plastic plants rustled as Fritz came to an exasperated stop behind her.

This was London's West End, through and through. Underneath a balcony on which theatre-goers could sip pre-show drinks was a huge, triangular marquee promoting the current performance – in this case, it was covered with the same stark, spotlit picture of Madame Gosselin as her flyer – and traced with a dazzling array of lights. This time, the curtained windows on the floors above weren't fake, though they were, fortunately for those holed up inside, inaccessible from the ground. Unlike Main Street, this wasn't just a front. The founders had actually built a complete theatre inside their resort, with each room by necessity functioning like its old-Earth counterparts.

Half a dozen men and women – both residents and workers, if their dirty clothes were anything to go by – gathered around its front doors. A couple of the younger members of the crowd were banging their fists against the brass and wood and broken panes of glass. Far from frustrated, they appeared to be enjoying the challenge. The doors had been chained and barricaded from floor to ceiling.

The two chatty locals Holly had been following stopped beside a muscular woman in a similar blue uniform to Fritz. The industrial power saw sat idly by her scuffed shoes. A thick, black cable ran from the device into a discrete plug socket by the corner of the theatre building. The woman grinned hungrily.

"What the hell is Zara doing with that lot?" Fritz hissed inches from her ear. Holly flinched. "She always seemed so... what's the word in English... demure."

"Really?"

"Well, it won't take her long to get through the door with that saw. We use that thing for cutting pipes. Can pretty much slice through the station's hull if you're not careful."

"Jesus, don't give these lunatics any ideas. So, the door's a no-go. How else do people get in and out of this place?"

"You keep forgetting I've never been here before. And if the survivors inside have barricaded the front door, what makes you think they haven't done the same with the maintenance tunnels as well?"

"Yeah, that's a good point. It looks like we can definitely throw the class-uprising hypothesis out the window, so some of the killers roaming the station must know their way around the behind-the-scenes infrastructure. Which means if they're still trying to cut their way through the front doors, they've almost certainly tried the access tunnels already."

"It also means the tunnels aren't as safe as we thought they were..."

Holly watched the locals continue to hammer gleefully at the barricade.

"There *has* to be another way in," she mused fretfully. "Maybe a route nobody inside or outside that place knows about. Nobody alive, that is."

"Sure." Fritz scoffed irritably. "Which means *we* don't know about it either, clever-clogs."

"Then think harder. Where else in this resort might have a connection to the theatre, staff who go where others don't?"

Fritz slowly brightened, lumen by lumen.

"The Convivium," he said. "It's a fancy restaurant on the other side of the district. Only place up here that's allowed to work with an open flame, so it provides the food for most of the residential sectors. I bet the bigwigs want dinner and a show sometimes, and there's no way the founders would allow waiters to openly carry hot dishes across the resort floor."

"Who's the clever-clogs now, eh?" Holly grinned at him. "Let's hope this restaurant's taking walk-ins."

CHAPTER
TWENTY

Fritz struggled with the paradox of both guiding Holly towards the Convivium and resisting her plan entirely. For every two steps he took towards the restaurant, he shuffled another fidgety metre back.

"Are you sure this is a good idea, Holly?" he whispered to her from behind a cast-iron bench just past the central fountain. "Even if we do find a way inside the theatre, then what? We can't get the people inside anywhere safer than they are right now."

"So, what do you suggest? We leave everyone to get cut apart by Zara and her massive buzzsaw?"

"Of course not! Just... well, I don't know. Don't you think we should stick to the plan? If I can fix the comm system, Flynn Industries can send a proper strike team in to stop this."

"By which point everyone inside the Andronicus will be insane or dead," Holly hissed. "Including my sister."

"Including *us*, if we're caught in there with them."

They paused behind the shrubbery outside the restaurant entrance.

"If it were Maria inside the Andronicus instead of my sister, would *you* leave her to be killed by that lot?" She huffed. "On second thought, maybe don't answer that."

"Hey." Fritz's face turned stoney. "Enough. I won't be made to feel guilty for being a realist. I'll help you find a way inside, but if we doom the lives of everyone on Saturnalia trying to save one person – that's on you."

He poked his head up from the bushes, ducked slightly as he spotted another pair of Saturnalians making their rounds of the resort floor, and then hesitantly emerged from cover.

"Looks clear out here," he whispered, nodding to the door. "Let's hope the, how you say, *bourgeoisie* haven't chosen this moment to take their lunch break, huh?"

He pushed open the restaurant door, standing to one side to let her pass as if he were the door staff who normally checked bookings at the podium outside. Holly suspected his chivalry was just a rouse to ensure she faced any potential danger before he did.

The fancy vestibule was circular, despite the restaurant's flat frontage, with a cloakroom on the left and a pair of bathrooms to the right. A handful of fur coats and dinner jackets still hung from the rails behind the counter. What use anyone found in a coat when the entire station was purposefully climate-controlled for comfort was beyond Holly, but then she remembered feeling a slight chill outside. Yet another fabrication. An artificial breeze had to be piped through the gardens of the resort to give residents the impression they were passing outside between attractions rather than stuck inside one giant, interstellar oil drum.

The inner doors were open, and Holly could see most of the marble-pillared restaurant even before the pair of them tiptoed through them. The Convivium had a varied seating plan – the booths closest to the centre of the grand hall were square and laid out in a grid, while the white-cloth tables towards the exterior walls were circular and came in all sizes, from cosy, romantic setups perfect for a couple to those suitable for parties of a dozen or more. Another bar, topped with an enormous art deco clock, resided in the very middle, though it boasted no stools around its counter. Table service only, Holly presumed, as one would expect from an establishment such as this – not that she'd ever frequented one before. It was evident a fight had broken out. Smashed martini glasses littered the bar and a couple of the tables had been overturned. Sheets had been pulled off and cast over the floor as if to cover up bodies at a crime scene.

She stuck her arm out to prevent Fritz from walking any further into the restaurant. They listened for the sound of cutlery clinking, of porcelain plates cracking, of baskets of stale bread crunching underfoot. Nothing, save for a gentle string accompaniment playing through speakers hidden in the hand-painted ceiling.

"Okay," she sighed. "I think we're alone. Reckon this service tunnel is gonna be in the kitchen?"

"I should think so. Either that or some kind of staff room or closet, or whatever, like in our canteen downstairs. There's no way they'd have waiters and porters coming and going through secret doors right here on the restaurant floor."

"Yeah, that was my thinking. Okay, let's spread out and see what we can find. Don't go out of sight, all right?"

"Don't worry. I won't make that mistake again."

Holly went left around the hall; Fritz took the route to the right. Their footsteps, no matter how carefully they stepped, were the only sounds – even the central clock appeared to have stopped ticking, though without her data pad Holly had no means of knowing whether it still told the correct time. She supposed it was all rather relative, anyway, given the station's lack of proper day and night cycle, not to mention the fact that it orbited a planet rather than the sun. If they calculated their years based on how long it took Titan to get round Saturn – fifteen days, by her understanding – everyone on board would be over a hundred by now.

One of the tables she passed still had plates of food on it, though even without flies to buzz around the decay Holly couldn't think of much else less appetising. Something had started off as eggs benedict, she reckoned, and since become a slush that was white where it should have been yellow and yellow where it should have been white. Another resident had ordered a fruit bowl full of strawberries that were now pink and black. At least the two glasses of mimosa still standing were roughly the colour and texture they ought to be. Holly believed the attack, or uprising, or whatever the tragic incident had been, had occurred around lunchtime, but she supposed if you owned the place you could order whatever you wanted, whenever you wanted – including the all-day brunch. Not long afterwards she accidentally stepped on the leftovers of numerous smørrebrød that had been knocked onto the floor. She hoped the congealed gunk plastered onto the neighbouring pillar was just a handful of tiramisu and not somebody's grey matter.

How long had it been since she last ate? She'd thrown up the sausage balls, but right now the sight of food made her feel queasy again rather than hungry. She knew she should keep her strength up, though, especially with rescue still days away – *if* they could send a message back home. The pantry of the Convivium had to be well stocked, she was sure, with food suitable for all sorts of tastes and cultures. Whether any of it hadn't spoiled was another matter entirely.

The overhead lights across the entire restaurant flickered on cue. Holly quickened her pace towards the kitchen doors. A total loss of power didn't exactly bode well for refrigeration.

Fritz disappeared in a clatter of crockery. Holly peered desperately over the central booths in the hope of discerning what had happened. Had one of the murderers been hiding under a table, waiting to strike? Had the floor given out? It looked fancy, but God knows how stable anything actually was behind the scenes. But then the dishevelled engineer picked himself back up, dusted the cake crumbs off his uniform, and offered her a pained and apologetic smile.

She rolled her eyes and continued through the restaurant, making a mental note to watch her step.

A pair of double doors – the sort that swing both inwards and outwards – separated the front of house from the kitchens and pantries and staff rooms. They were closed, and an anxious peek through their fingerprint-smeared windows hardly reassured Holly that no killers lay in wait on the other side. She backtracked from the doors, found a service trolley, and grabbed a steak knife from its tray.

Its dark wooden handle felt unnatural in her hand, brought back nauseating memories, but the last thing she wanted was a repeat of Dr. Humphrey's operating room...

Well, perhaps the second-to-last thing. The *truly* last thing she wanted was to be thrust into that situation again *without* a knife.

The door opened silently; she pushed through with her back to it and the shaking knife held out away from her in both hands. The putrid stench of spoiled meat wafted over her. Fritz followed with his fists raised; Holly wasn't sure which of them looked the least intimidating.

The kitchen was in far better state than that of the workers' canteen. Much bigger, too – whereas the canteen downstairs had room for five, maybe six kitchen staff at a push, this kitchen must have employed a team of two-dozen. Most of the pans still hung from hooks above the central stoves, though quite a few pots had either boiled their contents into a black, sticky residue or allowed the liquids inside to congeal into hard crusts. The air smelled sweet and pungent, and half the lights didn't work. A chopping board of thinly sliced raw fish had been left to fester. There was a brooding anticipation to the ambience – a sense that while nothing terrible had befallen the kitchen yet, it was only a matter of time before the inevitable happened.

No homicidal maniacs, though. Holly permitted her grip on the steak knife to relax slightly... but she wasn't prepared to drop it quite yet.

"Okay, get looking. The hatch was in the floor of the canteen's stockroom before, but the service tunnel for this place could be anywhere. Try to think outside the box, I guess."

"It might not even be hidden," Fritz suggested. "The kitchen's already behind the scenes."

"Let's hope so."

They scoured every inch of back-of-house. The only doors in the kitchen led to other sections of the restaurant. The fridge-freezer still worked, and Fritz held open the door so that Holly could explore it with her hands tucked under her armpits without getting locked inside. It was a frosty labyrinth of fish and poultry and hanging cow carcasses. No secret hatch. They checked the pantry next. Enough bags of rice to fill a swimming pool, mountains of pastas and flour, crates of wines and spirits and, much to Holly's surprise, oven chips... but no exit there, either. Expeditions into the office and stockroom were no more fruitful.

Growing desperate, they returned to the kitchen. Fritz tutted to himself as he ran his hands over the tiles. Holly felt a fist squeeze her heart, afraid he might demand they call off the search. She decided to keep him distracted.

"Hey, Fritz. You said you were from Germany, right?"

"Can't you tell from the accent?" he replied without turning around, as he prodded and probed a nondescript wall.

"What do you miss most about it?"

Fritz laughed and puffed out his cheeks.

"That's a tricky one. The food, maybe? I was never that big a schnitzel guy, but bratwurst? *Mein Gott*. Maria had to put me on a diet, my belly got so big. No," he said suddenly, brightening, "the beer! Proper German beer. The worker food here might be simple, and I'd kill for something authentic, but alcohol down on the lower levels is pretty much non-existent."

"Tell you what. We get off this station alive, and I'll buy the first round. How's that sound?"

"Hey, I won't say no to that! Of course, it'll have to be the good stuff. None of that synthetic crap..."

They both jumped as an earsplitting metallic screech flooded into the room from outside. Holly looked to the restaurant doors and back at Fritz, aghast.

"Is that the saw? Fuck. They've started already. Look harder!"

"Holly, come on..."

"I'm not giving up, Fritz! My sister's in there!"

Think, Holly, think. She spun around desperately, tears welling in her eyes. Fritz was right – there's no way the same people who refused to have maids and engineers walking down Main Street would allow waiters to openly carry their meals through the resort. There had to be a servants' passage of some kind. She just wasn't seeing it.

Come on, come *on*...

Stacks of baguettes on trays ready for cutting; sinks full to the brim with brown, murky water; a set of shelves with wheels at the bottom; leaning towers of bowls and plates and—

Wait. Her heart stopped. Why would a set of kitchen shelves need wheels?

She groped blindly amongst the bottles and boxes for a handle, found one, yanked it down. The shelves swung away from the wall with a drawn-out *shluck* sound. The door it masked was as thick as that of a bank vault, and its airlock-style frame capable of withstanding sudden depressurisation. A pearl-string of light bulbs flickered to life along a dark, narrow corridor. Fritz let out a bark of surprise and hurried inside.

"Ha. Smart." Holly admired the secret doorway with almost hysterical disbelief. "Let no space go wasted. I like it."

"Are you in a hurry to get there or not?" Fritz hissed from inside the alcove.

The shriek of the power saw kicked up again. Holly flinched.

"Listen to that thing. They'll break through the theatre door long before we get there."

Her eyes fell on the ovens.

"What would happen if we turned on all the stoves?"

"You would get flames, Holly. You have been in a kitchen before, yes?"

"Mine's electric," she replied sarcastically. "And what would happen if, say, the kitchen suddenly had a lot of flames at once? Like, more than the acceptable limit."

"Acceptable limit...?" The lines of Fritz's brow grew

deeper. "No, you're not suggesting we start a fire, Holly. We're on a space station. You'll get everyone killed!"

"What would happen, Fritz?"

"Well... I suppose the siren would go off, the fire suppression system would kick in – presuming this place still has any water pressure, that is – and then the immediate sector would go into lockdown like back in Laundry. The sector being the whole restaurant, I imagine."

"Sounds like a pretty damn good distraction, then."

She rushed back through the kitchen doors and into the restaurant.

"Holly, wait!" Fritz called after her impotently. "If the fire suppression and lockdown systems fail, the fire could rage through all of Saturnalia! You realise this station is just a big can of oxygen, don't you?"

"It won't spread if the people trying to break into the theatre put it out in time," she said, hurrying back with her arms full of tablecloths. "So let's hope they haven't all gone completely deranged."

She threw the tablecloths over the top of the ovens, spread them out so they covered as much space as possible. Then she tossed all the leftover bread baskets on top for good measure.

"I'm beginning to think you have," Fritz mumbled to himself, shrinking into the dark passageway.

Holly sprinted around the cluster of ovens, twisting every knob she could find. Some of them ignited the gas stoves – she had to push a few abandoned pans onto the floor, all the while wondering to herself why the rich needed their Cherries Jubilee so badly they'd risk total immolation – and within a few seconds patches of the tablecloths began to smoke and smoulder. She grabbed an open bottle of rum from the nearby counter and doused the pyre. The sudden explosion of heat singed the hairs on her arm yet sent shivers down her spine.

"This is not a good idea," Fritz whispered in horror as Holly backed away from the growing fire. "Do you really think this'll make them forget about the survivors inside the theatre?"

"It doesn't need to keep them distracted forever," Holly said as she pulled the vacuum-sealed door shut behind them. "Just long enough for us to get my sister out."

CHAPTER
TWENTY-ONE

The service tunnels resembled a mine shaft – dark and dirty, with slender pipes that dripped and discarded trolleys with silver cloches making already claustrophobic corridors an even tighter squeeze. Past the vacuum-sealed kitchen door lay a short set of steps, and then the passageways spread out to form a labyrinth. A whole subterranean network had operated directly beneath the resort floor without the wealthy up top ever realising.

Holly hated it. It wasn't just the foreboding sense of a collapse at any moment – it was stupid, she knew, given the steel beams were sturdier than any old-world rock face – but the dread that somebody – some*thing* – might be lurking down in the dungeons with them, poised to come running through the dark with sharp claws and salivating teeth.

Despite the very real horrors she'd already experienced in her short time aboard the Saturnalia, it was the gloomy unknown that made her feel like a little girl afraid of the monsters under her bed again.

And what horrors the mind could conjure...

They had no map and no sense of direction, losing their

bearings almost as soon as Holly shut the door behind them. Fortunately, the way to the Andronicus was clear. Rudimentary signs had been erected along the route, black stencilled font on cheap white plastic, pointing their staff towards whichever store or attraction they needed to reach.

Another set of steps marked their arrival at the theatre. Holly, who'd led their party of two at a breakneck pace despite her fear of the dark, rushed forward and gave the door at the top a push. It wouldn't give. She realised it was another security door designed to compartmentalise each section of the resort and protect the rest from unexpected depressurisation. A flat, thin handle was set into a groove shaped like a pie-quarter; she pushed it down, anti-clockwise, and the door hissed open.

Light swam in from the other side. Little else did. All was quiet – no talking, no footsteps against soft carpet, no music playing over the foyer speakers. Survivors or no survivors, the Andronicus felt as dead and deserted as the rest of the station.

"She's got to be here," Holly muttered to herself in a voice so quiet even she struggled to hear it. "She's *got* to be."

Fritz edged past her, enormous carving knife in hand.

"Where'd you get *that* from?" Holly asked.

"The kitchen, of course," he replied. "I grabbed it while you were busy setting fire to the place."

"Shit." She looked down at her empty hands. "I must have dropped mine while searching for the door."

"Oh well. I'm not sure they'll do much to stop a horde of crazed killers, anyway. Where in the theatre are we?"

"Beats me. I've never been in one before. You?"

"Not since I was very little."

The door had opened onto a back room of some kind. More service trolleys lined the wall, as did the odd usherette trays Holly had seen theatre staff wearing in old photographs. Was it normal, back then, to want ice cream during a pantomime? She suspected Saturnalia wasn't where she'd find the answer. Hessian sacks of corn; shelves of chocolates and sweets wrapped in transparent plastic like goldfish won at a fair. Cardboard boxes stacked into towers. A quick check inside the open flaps revealed hundreds more of the same black flyer she found back in Rosie's apartment.

"Hey, look." Fritz had cracked open a wooden door over by the corn sacks. "I think this is the foyer. Doesn't look like anyone's broken in yet. I guess your distraction worked."

Holly nudged him out of the way so she could see. The foyer was as lavish and decadent as the suites and atrium and everywhere else on the upper sectors of Saturnalia – the wonder she once felt at the sight of unimaginable riches had evolved into a boredom towards the expensive mundanity of it all. Polished brass, rich oak panels, fancy crystal chandelier... blah, blah, blah. She'd swap it all for a mud trench so long as her sister could be found at the end of it.

Past a ticket and concession stand – noticing the dried-out popcorn at the bottom of their machines, she now realised what the sacks of corn were for – was the inside of the theatre doors. Their wood was chipped, even broken through in places, and both the metal handles and chains used to keep them shut had been sheered through with something sharp. Every piece of furniture and rope-pole and rubbish bin not screwed to the floor had been shoved up against them.

They both jumped as a steady, vicious banging shook the doors. The precarious barricade shifted backwards, inch by inch.

"Erm, I may have spoken too soon," Fritz said, retreating. "Back into the service tunnel?"

"No, my sister's still in here!" Holly sprinted to the wooden door on the opposite side of the stock room. "We're not leaving without her!"

"You don't even know…" Fritz gritted his teeth and exhaled furiously. "Shit. You're going to get us killed."

"Not both of us," she said from inside the doorway. "*You* don't have to follow."

But, following a brief, panicked moment of hesitation while the kicking at the door got fiercer and fiercer, he did.

"Where do you think the survivors are?" he asked with tired resignation.

"Who the hell knows? I just hope we look marginally less dangerous than the people who are trying to kill them."

Fritz gingerly pointed at the blood splatters on her shirt.

"Are you sure about that?"

"Well, Rosie will recognise me. It's up to the others if they want to follow us to safety or not."

The back door had taken them to a curved corridor circling the auditorium – the gold print above the double doors closest to them read STALLS. Holly went to push through them, presuming they weren't barricaded like the front doors. If she were trapped inside a theatre while the rest of a space station went homicidally insane, where would she hide? Somewhere backstage, probably. And the best way of getting backstage, given she hadn't the slightest inkling how to navigate the crew corridors, was by rushing past the lowest level of seats and crossing the stage itself.

But as she approached the doors, she heard a great calamitous crashing sound from back inside the foyer. The barricade was breached… and judging by the heavy footsteps coming their way, the killers outside had a similar idea to her.

"Up the corridor," she snapped at Fritz. "Move!"

They sprinted in the opposite direction to the foyer, past a set of bathroom doors, until they reached a staircase. Up they went, swinging into the long, glittery bar whose balcony overlooked the gardens of the resort floor, before reaching the set of stairs on the opposite side and climbing another storey. UPPER CIRCLE was written above the final flight and BOXES marked a doorway on the landing halfway up. Not entirely sure what either descriptor meant, Holly grabbed Fritz's hand and pulled him through the latter. Every corridor looked like the last. She threw open a random door on her right, spotted the dimly lit stage below, and barrelled them both inside. The four seats were bolted to the floor of the box, but the stand for the champagne bucket wasn't. She used it to wedge the door shut. She doubted it would withstand much force, but hopefully it would be enough that anyone on the other side would believe the door was locked and move on.

They squatted between the chairs and the balcony wall and waited for deranged death to catch up to them. But the only doors that got kicked open were the ones back down in the stalls. Zara marched through first, massive rescue saw still in hand, revving it like a motorbike engine, followed by her gaggle of grinning maniacs, who sprinted past her down the aisles flanking the seats towards the wooden boards of the stage.

Zara threw the saw into the stalls, kicked the back of the rearmost seat, and let out a triumphant laugh.

"Get out here," she yelled. "The show's about to start!"

The other maniacs flowed past the curtains draped in the wings. Holly heard gasps and shrieks moments later. She gripped the edge of the balcony, bit right through her bottom lip, and watched as they returned dragging various men and women onto the stage – most in evening dress, a couple in usher uniforms.

"That's Rosie." Holly felt the world fall from under her. "Shit, that's Rosie right there!"

She stood up and headed for the box's door. Fritz threw her back down again.

"What the hell are you doing?" he hissed in her face. "If you go out there now, they'll kill you!"

"They'll kill *Rosie*, Fritz!"

She tried to push him off her, but he grabbed both of her wrists together and held firm.

"I don't care what happened between you two. I'm pretty sure she doesn't want to share a reunion with your severed head!"

"But—"

"But nothing! Shut up! The best and only thing you can do right now is keep *stumm* and pray."

Screw prayer. If there was a God, he certainly hadn't been keeping an eye on Saturnalia. If the psychopaths downstairs wanted to kill Rosie, they would, and nobody – not God, not Holly, not the full might of the UEC marine corp – was going to stop them.

"Fuck," she spat, clenching her jaw so hard her molars hurt.

Two of the men and one of the women who'd been dragged out were bleeding from head wounds. They looked sluggish, detached, as if they didn't realise the severity of their situation. The rest were terrified. Rosie wore a sheer, split-thigh dress covered almost as much by sequins as it was by a film of sweat and dirt. Her mascara streaked down her cheeks. She still kept a tight grip on her tiny clutch purse as if it were some kind of forcefield keeping the monsters at bay. Holly believed it was her husband, Lewis, crouching beside her – it was hard to recognise him from his pictures with his nose so badly broken.

The attackers formed a perimeter around the battered, bloodied group, laughing and twirling their instruments, blunt and sharp alike.

"We don't want any trouble," an old man with a bushy grey moustache said, his words wavering. "Just... Just pay us no mind, won't you? Whatever happened out there – we want no part in it, you hear me?"

"No part in it?" Zara let out a goggle-eyed laugh. "But you're already in it. We all are! And, well, if you didn't want to play your part, Mr. Galanis, why are you sitting out here on a stage?"

The mob tittered like naughty school girls. Mr. Galanis opened his mouth to reply, made a series of unintelligible, disgruntled babbling sounds instead, and shrank shamefully back into the crowd of survivors.

She clapped her hands together.

"As it teaches us, those who open their eyes are rewarded. Those who turn from the light are blind... and this flock cannot afford to be led astray by liars and heretics."

"We've done nothing wrong!" a tearful young woman in an usher's uniform shouted.

"But that doesn't mean you've done anything right, either, does it?" Zara mused jovially. "And we have given you plenty of opportunities. *Plenty*."

She addressed the unstable members of her audience.

"What do we do to those who refuse the light?"

"We string them up," the mob recited as one, "so that they may see it better."

Zara gestured to the horrified group.

"Well, get to it, then."

Everybody screamed as the attackers closed in. They

grabbed Mr. Galanis, who could only put up the feeblest of fights against his two younger assailants. Holly gasped as another pair strode towards Rosie... only to grab the arms of Lewis Flynn instead. He was slightly more successful at resisting. He swung a fist at a crazed janitor's face, then shoulder-barged into a man in a bloodstained tuxedo, before a club to the back of his legs sent him crashing to his knees. Rosie let out a cry and tried to help him, only to receive a swift backhand from a third psychopath. Bleeding from her mouth and with the arms of another wealthy woman wrapped around her shoulders, she watched and whimpered as her husband was dragged away.

"Don't," Fritz hissed as Holly tried to rush to her sister's rescue again. "You'll only make it worse!"

The other members of the mob had already prepared nooses from the stage rigging. They slipped the ropes around the necks of the two victims while their Oxford shoes scraped black skid marks across the waxed boards. Then, their laughter drowning out even the most terrified of cries, they heaved on the pulleys and lowered the sandbag counterweights. Lewis Flynn and Mr. Galanis were slowly pulled up towards the fly loft, spluttering and spitting and scratching at the ropes while their feet performed a desperate tap dance.

Then they left the floor, and their faces turned from pink to purple.

Rosie let out a tragic wail like a wounded animal. Holly gritted her teeth and gripped the balcony railing so hard that one of her fingernails bent back. She realised she was crying as a tear dripped off her cheek and splattered against the dark fabric of her trousers. She wanted desperately to rush down there, to throw her arms around her sister and tell her that now they were together again, everything would be all right... but she knew that what Fritz said was true. To do so would not only get herself and Fritz killed, but increase the odds of Rosie meeting the same fate as well.

She released a quiet, high-pitched whimper and let her head sink to her knees. This was too much to bear. When she raised her head again, her brother-in-law's legs had stopped kicking. Mr. Galanis suffered one last violent, involuntary death-spasm, and then he too was still.

Zara clapped her hands together again.

"What do you reckon, friends? Surely they can see the truth from up there!"

The mob nodded enthusiastically. Her face grew stoney as she turned back to the remaining survivors.

"So. Who's next?"

"No!" One of the other flush gentlemen clasped his hands together and begged. "Please, no! We're ready to see the light, the truth – all of it!"

"We were wrong to resist," said the woman with her arms around Rosie. "It's clear now. We should have sided with you from the start."

Zara eyed the group with pantomime suspicion.

"And do you *all* feel this way?"

"Yes," Rosie gurgled through a veil of blood, phlegm and tears. "I want to understand."

A moment of silence filled the auditorium – such a perfect silence that Holly was sure the assorted murderers would hear her thudding heart. Then Zara spread her arms out wide.

"That's all we wanted to hear, friends! I can see the belief glinting in your eyes. *You. Are. Ready!* On your feet, people. It's time to meet the menhir."

The mob ushered the survivors towards the doors to the foyer. Holly and Fritz ducked beneath the wall of the balcony before anyone could spot them. Fritz raised a trembling finger to his lips. Holly kept flexing and opening her hands with her eyes scrunched tight until she heard the doors of the theatre *thunk* shut again.

"Fuck. Fuck!" Holly stood up and ran her hands through her hair as she paced back and forth across the box. "They've got Rosie, Fritz! What the hell am I supposed to do?"

"I don't know," he admitted, desperately scanning the auditorium for any killers who'd stayed behind. "But Holly – your sister is alive! Isn't that brilliant? We'll figure something out. Well... we'll send for help, right?"

"Yeah." She felt like she was sitting at the bottom of a deep, dark well again. "Shit. Yeah. I guess we'll do that."

"Stay strong, Holly." Fritz grabbed her arms; she was surprised by how bright and optimistic his eyes were. "Honestly, I didn't think your sister would be here. But she was! And that means... well, I don't want to sound foolish, but..."

"But maybe Maria is still alive, too."

"Exactly! Exactly." He let go of her and pried open the box's door. "And if she is, we're going to find her. And then the four of us are getting off this tin fucking powder-keg together."

"Okay. Yeah." Holly kept nodding. "Everything's gonna be okay."

But for some reason, watching her sister's late husband dangle above the stage, she didn't think it would be.

CHAPTER
TWENTY-TWO

Retracing their steps to the stockroom of the theatre's foyer was too risky, but fortunately an alternative service tunnel was close by. Holly had to rush into one of the bathrooms next door to the box to throw up and, while emptying what little contents her stomach still possessed into the grand, round communal basin beside the stalls, discovered a small hillock of mops and buckets piled up against the tiles on the far wall. She and Fritz disassembled the barricade and discovered another hidden door leading back down into the catacombs beneath the resort floor.

"We'll follow it all the way to Administration," Fritz said enthusiastically as he secured the door behind them. "I'm sure the people up in the Observation gallery need food delivered, too."

Apparently not, as it turned out. Following the bare, plastic signs in the subterranean labyrinth, and after an accidental detour that very nearly took them up onto the sandless shores of Prosperity Bay, they reached another industrial

207

door marked GRAND STAIRWAY – and there the path ended. No rickety elevator or dilapidated stairwell leading them up to the sector above. Just a door.

"Perhaps they don't trust us workers scurrying around behind all the important stuff," Fritz wondered aloud, his newfound optimism only marginally dampened. "Doesn't matter. The Resort District and Operations are interconnected anyway."

He went to unseal the door. Holly reached out and grabbed his hand.

"Be careful," she whispered. "We don't know where those bastards took Rosie and the rest. The resort could have cleared out, or every psychopath on Saturnalia might be right outside."

His fingers lingered on the flat paddle-handle. He swallowed hard and nodded.

"Yes. Yes, we'll take it slow."

Down the handle went. A slurpy sucking noise. The sleepy groan of neglected hinges. Through the growing gap they saw luscious palm trees, glittery statues, even a poster for something involving a giant pink elephant... but no unhinged residents on patrol. Wherever Rosie had been taken, it seemed like nobody else wanted to miss the show.

"There's the staircase," Fritz whispered, waving Holly through. "We'd better be quick while it's quiet. Once we're on the steps, we'll be completely exposed."

Holly pointed numbly to the ceiling.

"Like her, you mean?"

The young, female usher from the Andronicus had been hanged from a towering archway of flowers. She'd been stripped of her uniform and the words *do you see?* had been finger-painted across her bare chest and stomach in blood.

"Fucking monsters," Fritz gasped. "She must have tried to run after they left the theatre..."

Holly's breathing grew sharp and erratic. She reached out and held onto the wall to keep from fainting. Fritz hurried back, arms outstretched like a confused orangutan in case he needed to catch her.

"Hey," he said. "Look at me. That's not Rosie, which means she's still alive, right? I need you to keep it together, for both our sakes. For Rosie's... for Maria's. Can you do that?"

"Yeah, I can do that, just..." She brushed him off. "Don't crowd me, all right? I just... I still can't get over how fucking horrible this all is. I came here to rescue my sister from an unhealthy relationship, not a horde of homicidal zealots."

"Yeah, this isn't exactly how I saw the end of my week going, either."

The grand stairway put even the steps of the Welcome Lobby to shame. It flared out at its top and bottom like an hourglass, and a carpet red enough for Hollywood lolled past it into the resort like a long, fat tongue. Saturnalia's trademark spotlights flanked it on either side, slowly and gracefully tilting forwards and back (one of the four had locked in position, presumably due to the station's gradual loss of power). Every visible trim was adorned with rubies and sapphires the size of golf balls, each pilfered from the old mines of Earth.

The two of them raced up the stairs, keeping to the soft carpet rather than the hard marble, glancing alternately over their shoulders at the resort gradually disappearing behind them and up towards the top of the stairs. The massive entrance to Operations & Observation beckoned beyond – almost completely circular like a gigantic porthole, the jewelled glitz that framed it acted as the resort's last bastion against the next sector's distinct rejection of excess and opulence.

Everything in Operations – which formed the bulk of the topmost sector, with Observation just a single (albeit popular) component – was bathed in spotless, sterile white. Every door was as circular as that through which they just entered. Even the ceiling was white, featureless, and, even now, so well-kept that it was almost impossible to tell how far or close to the observer it actually was. A faint electrical hum permeated the air, compensating for the total lack of aroma. If the rest of the station was Saturnalia's heart, stuck resolutely in the past, Operations was its brain, with eyes only for the future.

Pretty much the only thing not white, save for the light grey trim outlining each doorframe, skirting board and vent grille, was the trail of dirty footprints and droplets of blood that stretched from the resort towards the giant disc-like doors at the far end.

"Do you recognise this sector?" Holly whispered to Fritz. Even with her voice kept to a minimum, the words reverberated around the empty, plastic halls like lottery balls inside a tombola. "You said you once came up here to fix an issue with external maintenance, right?"

"Yeah, years ago. I remember how clean everything looks. Not sure I can say I know my way around, though."

"Can you get us to Administration?"

"Administration? Well, that's easy."

He pointed at the door to their left. ADMINISTRATION was clearly printed on a bronze plaque beside it.

"I reckon it might be that one," he said.

"All right, smart-arse." Holly smiled apprehensively. "Let's see you fix this comms array, shall we?"

The circular door automatically split in half upon their approach. Once again, Holly was shocked by the disparity between the modernity of the Operations sector and the anachronistic illusion the residents of Saturnalia chose to immerse themselves within. This was closer to the aesthetic she'd witnessed aboard the Arks that evacuated Earth – economical, efficient and grounded in the technologies of today. She had to remind herself that the people operating these sections of the station were still staff, still somewhat tethered to reality, even if they enjoyed a better life than the unfortunate grunts crammed together down in Engineering.

The room beyond was like the bridge of a battlecruiser – all computer terminals and touch-screen monitors and more bleeping lights than was probably healthy. There was even a lone chair elevated above all the rest towards the back – the workstation assigned to Andrew Yang, if Holly had to hazard a guess. Most of the monitors were either switched off, smashed and cracked, or showed nothing but a grainy static image, but a few of the two-dozen screens mounted like a panoramic tapestry on the wall relayed high-definition feeds of various parts of the space station. Holly recognised shots from the atrium, Main Street and the resort floor directly outside the Convivium, and felt a rush of relief that nobody had still been around to watch them.

Fritz hurried over to Yang's computer and woke it up by tapping the enter key.

"It's password protected. Administrator access only."

"You're kidding me. There's only a single computer that can control Saturnalia, and it's locked to one man's account?"

"We should count ourselves lucky it doesn't require biometrics. Any guesses?"

Holly doubled over with her head in her hands and groaned.

"Fine. Put in 'saturnalia'. And 'password'. You know, the obvious ones."

"Nope."

"Try 'rich people are great'. All one word."

"*Mein Gott*, it worked!"

Holly shot bolt-upright.

"Really?"

"Of course not! This is perhaps the wealthiest cabal humanity has ever produced – do you really think they didn't implement a half-decent security system?"

"Fuck. I thought you were good with computers and stuff?"

"I'm an electrical engineer, not a hacker!"

"So, what are you saying? You can't even turn this thing on?"

"Don't be—" Fritz grunted and shook his head. "Give me a moment. I might be able to reboot it in safe mode or something, access some of the essential systems."

Holly didn't know which combination of keys Fritz held down next, but it sure looked like hacking to her. The once bright, blue-tinged screen went dark, and the next thing she knew he was clicking his way through a black and white digital landscape that would have looked out of date half a century ago. He licked his lips in concentration. She left him to it.

Everything in the control centre seemed to make odd *beeps* and *boops*. She didn't know if they were supposed to, or if each irritating noise indicated yet another part of Saturnalia that was falling to pieces. Mother had always told her to learn how computers worked. Said it would keep her in good stead, the way humanity was replacing everything with machines. Well, it sure would have come in handy now.

Nestled amongst the server units was a row of locked doors. Holly punched the button beside the closest one and it hissed up into the ceiling. A long, narrow walkway lay on the other side. Three large, identical orbs sat in pockets to either side of it.

"Erm, Fritz?" She slowly retreated towards him and tapped him on the shoulder. "What are those?"

Fritz glanced behind him, blinked twice, and then his eyes doubled in size.

"Are those the escape pods?"

"What, you *knew* about these? And you didn't think to mention them before? We had another way off this station *all this time?*"

"I've never actually seen them, Holly! I... I didn't even know they were real! This may surprise you, but the workers aren't exactly high on the founders' list of evacuees in emergencies like this. Besides, I would have assumed they'd been used already."

"Clearly they haven't!"

"Yes, but look. See those sparking control panels? The release mechanisms on the first two are busted. They likely haven't been used because the madmen who took over the station sabotaged them."

"Maybe not all of them," Holly said desperately, opening the other doors along the rear wall. Six more pods rested in each, for a grand total of eighteen.

Not enough for every resident of Saturnalia to reach freedom – not by a large margin – but then again, the naval architects of the Titanic hadn't thought it needed lifeboats, either.

"Right. I'm in." Fritz waved her over. "Most of the security commands are off-limits without Yang's login details, but I can get readouts from some of the more basic admin features."

"What about comms? Can you run a diagnostic on the issue from here?"

Fritz navigated the list of folders and commands. It had been a long time since he used a computer like this, and it showed. After much swearing and backtracking, he shook his sorry head.

"No, it hasn't been disabled on this end. From what this tells me, this is no firmware issue, and nobody has switched the comm system off from here. The array itself is broken, I think – which somebody would have to do from outside the station. Either that or something else is blocking the messages from getting through."

"External maintenance," Holly sighed. "That EVA pod. They must have gone out there to damage the array and cut Saturnalia off from the rest of the galaxy."

"I know I'm an engineer," Fritz said apologetically, "but there's no way I'm fixing that."

"That's okay. I doubt it can be fixed. They destroyed Laundry just to get at us. I can't imagine there's much of an array left."

They fell into an anaesthetised silence. With the shuttle out of action, and the comms on Saturnalia permanently offline, there was no way to alert Flynn Industries or the UEC military. Nobody was coming to their rescue – not until the next squad of oblivious marines came to check on them, that is. Fritz continued to explore the features available to them in safe mode, the keys clacking enthusiastically, until his fingers stopped moving and he hooted in surprise.

"I wasn't sure if this would work," he said. "Maria once told me that all of the residents on board Saturnalia wore these bracelet things – kind of like those old fitness trackers, you know? It was so people couldn't get lost, but also so Administration could monitor people's biometric readouts and send out a medical team if somebody fell ill suddenly. I never saw the bracelets myself, not really seeing any of the residents and all, but Maria, being a maid, well..."

"Where are you going with this, Fritz?"

"Well, I can't access the biometric details – I think it's only listing residents with a heartbeat, anyway – and the full station map is only available with Yang's login, and Yang doesn't appear to be on the list, as far as I can see, which probably means he's—"

"Fritz?"

"I can see where everybody is," Fritz hurriedly explained. He moved aside so Holly could see the screen better. "Everybody with a tracking bracelet, at any rate. I've found Rosie." He deflated slightly. "Shame it doesn't show where Maria is, of course..."

As Fritz said, safe mode didn't offer a proper map of Saturnalia. As such, all of the surviving residents were just listed in a column along with the sector in which they were presently located. Holly frantically scanned the list until she found her sister.

"She's in the Gallery." She tapped the screen excitedly. "In fact, almost *everyone* seems to be in either the Gallery or the Observation deck. I suppose that makes sense, right?" she asked Fritz. "They probably still think they killed us back in Laundry, and the last of the survivors were holed up in the theatre. All of the locals are congregating in the same place now their purge is complete."

"Yes. Unfortunately, it's the same place where they have your sister. And Maria, hopefully, unless she had better luck at keeping hidden."

Holly turned to him, concerned.

"And what if Maria is, you know, insane like the rest of them? What will you do?"

Fritz mulled this over, then smiled weakly. The poor man looked older and more tired than ever.

"Then I suppose I'll have to go a little crazy, too."

TWENTY-THREE

They left ADMINISTRATION. Four other circular doors beckoned them.

"Please tell me we aren't going in that direction," Holly said, eyeing the trail of dirt and blood.

"No, that's Observation," Fritz replied. "The gallery is just over—"

They heard voices coming up the stairs from the resort. Fritz grabbed Holly's arm and pulled her towards the nearest disc-shaped door – the one marked EXTERNAL MAINTENANCE. They disappeared from view just as two dishevelled men finished their climb and marched into Operations.

"Gas leak, d'ya reckon?" one of them asked.

"Could be," replied the other. "Seems every pipe is either empty or overloaded. Father says we'll have to fix things now the heretics are all rounded up."

"Well, at least the fire's out. Restaurant sector's on lockdown now, though. You know, I don't think I've eaten in days—"

The half-doors of external maintenance clamped shut, cutting off the rest of their conversation. Holly shuddered.

The directory on Yang's computer hadn't shown anyone down in the resort. Well, nobody with a tracking bracelet. She guessed they'd been staff members before they lost their minds.

External Maintenance was closer to a laboratory than it was the industrial rats nest of Engineering. Much as the Residential District tried to convince tenants that they were back on some misremembered version of Earth, the vents of External Maintenance were so hidden and the white walls so soundproofed that you could forget you were actually on the top floor of a space station orbiting Saturn – one that was close to tearing itself apart. A quick search for enemies revealed it consisted of multiple rooms, each sealable against contamination and depressurisation, beginning with tech-desks and culminating in the docking bay for the EVA pod. Presently they found themselves surrounded by microscopes and vacuum chambers and the kind of computer setups a Flynn Industries office worker could only dream of.

Holly sagged onto the emptiest desk she could find.

"That was too close," she said, "and that was only two of them. There must be dozens of people between us and Rosie. We'll never make it to her without getting captured. Or killed."

Fritz passed into the EVA pod's docking bay and gestured irritably for Holly to follow. She did so.

"What are you saying?" he asked once they were safely out of sight of any murderers who might wander into the sector. "That you want to, what? Leave her to her fate?"

"No, of course not," she replied. She bowed her head, unable to look Fritz in the eye. "I just don't see how we can help her."

"This whole time you've been pushing to save this woman, lying to me about who you are and why you came here, fighting any suggestion I made about finding my wife..."

"Hey, come on, that's not fair..."

"...and now, as soon as you see a way off this sinking ship, you're giving up?"

"I'm not giving up," Holly shouted, before quickly lowering her voice. "I'm trying to stay alive, Fritz. There's a difference. I never lied about my job. I *am* an analyst. So trust me when I say there is no fucking way we're getting to Rosie *and* escaping in one piece. These whack jobs have murdered or indoctrinated or done God knows what else to everyone on Saturnalia, and if we go after Rosie they'll do the same to us. You saw how many escape pods there were. There must be a few that still work. Or you could fix the firing mechanism, or whatever. So long as we can eject from the station, we're safe, and maybe we can send a message back home once we're far enough out. Hell, the pod's distress beacon alone will be enough for Flynn to send another security team our way."

Fritz took a long look at her. He seemed to be chewing on what he wanted to say, deliberating whether he should share something with her or not, and eventually settled on marching off to the lobster-clawed bathysphere instead.

"A beautiful piece of engineering," he said, running his hand along its chipped and scraped exterior. "And another potential escape plan. But its comms are tied to Saturnalia, and it only operates within a short range of the station. Still, nobody here could ever reach you. You could drift outside until you ran out of air or food."

Holly approached him uneasily.

"Fritz?"

"If you want to leave, I won't stop you. Take an escape pod. Take the EVA. If you think you could live with yourself, then maybe you should. But I won't be going with you. I spent days hiding down in Engineering, assuming my wife was dead. I gave up on her because I was afraid – not just of dying as well, but of confirming my worst fears. I was certain that what I believed was true. But then we saw your sister, Holly, and her tracking bracelet shows she's still alive, and for the first time in days I actually feel *hope*. I was a coward. Worse than that – I was a bad husband. But if your sister is alive, Maria might be too. And if so, I'm sure as hell not leaving without her."

"Then you might not leave at all."

"So be it."

Holly chewed her lip.

"It's been eight years. If she wanted me here, she would have called – it's not like her husband couldn't afford to pay for the trip..."

Fritz finally tore his attention away from the EVA pod.

"It could be a lifetime, Holly. You're her sister. Of course she wants to see you."

Holly balled her hands into fists and produced a frustrated guttural noise deep in her throat.

"Fuck. Yeah, you're right. I'm just... I'm just scared, you know? If reuniting with Rosie wasn't terrifying enough, her husband just got strung up from the theatre rafters and a swarm of maniacs want to keep us apart. It's a little more than I bargained for."

"Hey, you tricked a multinational company into flying you across half a dozen star systems just so you could convince your sister to come home with you. Something tells me you're braver than you think."

"Yeah, or stupider." She pinched the bridge of her nose. "Right. Shit. If we're gonna do this, we need to do it smart. The arseholes won't let anyone from the theatre out of their sight again. We need to figure out a way of passing right under their noses without them noticing."

Fritz clicked his fingers and pointed to a row of lockers in which lean white spacesuits hung.

"We could wear these, maybe? We know they've sent people out in the EVA before. The helmets might hide our faces a bit."

"Yeah, but we don't know those lunatics even bothered putting a suit on, do we? And these suits are designed to reflect as much light as possible in case the user finds themselves floating out in space in need of rescue. I reckon these'll make us stand out even more."

Fritz sat down on the changing bench. A toolbox lay open beside it; he plucked out a large wrench and weighed the tool in his palm before tucking it into the back of his overalls.

"Well, that's my suggestion. That or we go back to sneaking – it's worked this far. You got any better ideas?"

Holly gave herself a minute to think.

"The residents and workers rarely ever saw one another, right?"

"Yeah. Except for some of the customer-facing staff, I guess. Why?"

"Well, I know it's been a few days since the social structure of this place got turned upside down, but the zealots out there can't possibly recognise *everyone*, right? So maybe we don't need to hide. Maybe we just need to fit in."

"Huh. You mean, walk around like we're one of them? Twirling fire pokers like batons and stuff?" Fritz nodded thoughtfully. "Could work. Risky, but..."

Holly bent down and grabbed a hammer from the toolbox. It had a nice swing to it.

"Yeah. And we need to grin. Grin like we fucking *mean it.*"

CHAPTER
TWENTY-FOUR

With the minimalistic intersection of Operations deserted once more, Holly and Fritz strolled out of External Maintenance with petrified grins plastered across their faces. The expression didn't come naturally. Holly felt less like laughing and more like crying, and already the muscles in her cheeks were starting to hurt. Talk about unhinged – it felt as if her jaw would fall off completely.

"Ready?" she whispered to Fritz, barely moving her lips.

"Not in the slightest," he replied, nervously passing his carving knife from hand to hand. "Are you sure we can't go back to sneaking?"

"Let's see how tight security is," she said as they approached the GALLERY door.

Its two halves slid open. Relative darkness waited on the other side. Gone were the white walls, replaced by ravines formed of purple curtains and squares of wood, three metres by three, funnelling guests forward. The gallery wasn't quite as dim as the most neglected nooks in Engineering, or the corridors where the light fixtures were broken or starved of power, but here it was controlled, rationed, used only to highlight and amplify. They passed into a pocket of stale air that evoked old libraries and unopened drawers.

They slowly weaved through a maze of cascading curtains and perpendicular display boards. Holly felt like she was being threaded back and forth through a loom. As she passed paintings even the most artistically illiterate of ex-Earthers could recognise – and, intermittently, sculptures inside tall glass cabinets, from balloon-themed pop art to marbled classics – the knot in her chest grew tighter, then snapped altogether.

"These aren't replicas," she whispered in awe. "Some of the most famous works of art ever made are in here."

"Self-contained module," Fritz explained breathlessly. "I've heard the gallery can detach from the rest of the space station entirely if necessary. To protect humanity's history, you know. Or maybe just the founders' investments."

"Would have been nice to know this stuff was here before I set fire to the kitchen, Fritz."

"You weren't in a particularly... *considerate* mood," he said through an increasingly pained grin.

Andy Warhol's *Gold Marilyn Monroe*. Vincent van Gogh's *Cafe Terrace at Night*. Rembrandt's *The Storm on the Sea of Galilee*.

"Hey..." Holly frowned and gave the last piece a double-take. "I thought that painting was stolen in—"

They both jumped out of their skin as they rounded the corner and came face to face with a pantsuit-wearing admin worker coming the opposite way. Her fists dripped with fresh blood. Quite unalarmed herself, she eyed them with bubbly curiosity.

"Do I know you?" she rasped, tilting her head.

Holly's first instinct was to run back the other direction.

Instead, she leaned forwards and forced herself to meet her steely gaze.

"Do I know *you?*"

She stared into the woman's watery, bloodshot eyes and tried desperately not to think of her would-be murderer back in the doctor's operating room. Holly's fingers tightened around her hammer. She was sure the woman would see through her fine-china mask and bury her fist three inches into the face behind it. But then she let out a playful giggle.

"Make sure you're in Observation in twenty. Father wants everyone upstairs for the Enlightenment."

She strolled past them towards the intersection in Observation, whistling as she went. Holly sucked in dusty air and fought the urge to hyperventilate.

"I can't believe that worked," Fritz said, finally letting out the breath he'd been holding.

"It won't a second time. Let's find Rosie and the others before any more of our friendly neighbours try making conversation."

They quickened their pace. Holly stopped paying the artwork any attention. She suspected she could spend days studying the exhibits, and by the sound of it, they only had a few minutes left to find Rosie and escape.

"What do you think she meant by enlightenment?" Fritz asked, unable to keep his nervousness to himself.

"No idea. Honestly, I'd really rather not find out."

They stopped speaking. Holly got the impression the circular route was taking them around the outskirts of the Gallery before slowly coiling towards its centre like an ammonite. She also suspected that they could take a shortcut and bypass much of the artwork simply by pushing their way through the dense curtains that blocked their view to either side, but she was afraid to get lost or stuck... or to run into more friendly neighbours than the two of them could handle with big smiles and words alone.

They reached the centre of the gallery. If there had once been a central exhibit on display in the spotlight clearing, no trace of it but its enormous, shatterproof-glass cube remained. The survivors from the theatre sat huddled inside it, as did a number of others abducted from elsewhere around the station. About two dozen in total. Holly almost dropped her hammer in her haste to sprint over.

"Rosie?" The inhabitants shrank back as she banged against the glass. "Rosie Bloom? Flynn, I mean. Somebody tell me where Rosie is!"

"Please don't hurt us," a young man begged. "We've done everything you've asked."

Though there was ample space to stand, a woman crawled forwards through the crowd on her hands and knees. It took Holly a few seconds to recognise her through the dry blood caked across her cheeks.

"Holly?" Rosie blinked at her blankly. "What are you doing here?"

Holly broke into a tearful smile.

"I came to take you home, Sis."

"Home? I thought I *was* home..." Rosie stared at the floor. "Oh, maybe not. How are we getting there?"

Fritz circled the cage, craning his neck to see over everyone, calling out Maria's name. The same woman who Holly had seen put her arm around Rosie's shoulders back in the theatre cautiously approached the glass.

"She's in shock. Her husband... well, she just lost him. Are you really here to rescue us?"

"Do you have a way off Saturnalia?" a man in another blue engineer's uniform asked, his hands splayed over the window as if he could push himself through. His wrists were tied together with rope.

"I can't find her," Holly heard Fritz mutter to himself in mounting panic. "She isn't here."

"I... I don't know." Holly struggled to look the other survivors in the eye. "We're still figuring all that out."

More of them pushed forward, drowning Rosie in the surge, all of their hands bound and pressing against the glass. Their questions clambered over one another. Fritz continued his desperate, futile search.

"I can't find her, Holly."

"Maybe she's still out there hiding, yeah? Please, everyone – be quiet!"

They only grew louder and more hopeless. Holly checked the way back out of the gallery. Half of Saturnalia could be charging back towards them and they'd never know.

"Fritz, help me get this door open. We need to get Rosie out of here before this lot alert the locals."

"But Maria *has* to be here, she—"

"Fritz, *please!*"

Fritz pulled out the master key they stole from the reception desk back at the residential suites, but he may as well have selected his socket wrench. As he went to try it in the lock, the door swung open quite freely.

"Something's not right," he said uneasily. "It's not even locked."

"Because they know everyone's too afraid to leave," Holly said, barging past him.

"But you said they wouldn't let them out of their sight..."

Everyone shrank back again once Holly entered the exhibit. She looked down at the hammer in her hand, at the bloodstains splashed against her shirt, at the knife trembling in Fritz's grip. Yeah, fair enough. They may have dropped the grins, but as far as the rest of the survivors were concerned, Holly and Fritz looked no different to everyone else.

"Cut Rosie's ties, will you?" she asked Fritz, before kneeling down beside her sister – the only survivor who wasn't now crowded against the opposite side of the cube. "Come on, Rosie. I'm here now. I'll keep you safe."

"Will Mum and Dad be there?" Rosie asked, smiling up at her. "At home, I mean. It's been a very long time, hasn't it?"

Holly shared a glance with Fritz, who resumed sawing at the rope.

"Yeah, Sis. Mum and Dad are waiting for us. Everything's going to be all right, I promise."

The knife finally broke through the last of the rope. Holly helped Rosie to her feet and then back through the door of the display – it was like dragging one of the theatre's hessian corn sacks – while Fritz went back to peering behind the curtains flanking the rest of the exhibit.

"Come on, Fritz," Holly hissed. "The locals will be back any second."

"I can't leave yet," he snapped. "Not until I know she's safe. She's here, I know it. I *know* it. I just have to find her."

Though some of the survivors had gone back to sitting on the floor, a few had summoned enough courage to follow them out of the giant display.

"Take us with you," they pleaded.

"You've got a ship, right?" another asked.

"She isn't here, Fritz," Holly tried to backtrack and grab him, but Rosie was too heavy. "Please! I can't get her out of here without you!"

"And I can't get out of here without my Maria!" He stared at her, his eyes brimming with tears. "Can't you understand that? She's all I have – and if Rosie is here, Maria must be too! She *must* be!"

A high-pitched cackle filled the gallery. Everybody froze. Well, Holly and Fritz did – the three survivors who'd followed them out of the glass exhibit slowly crept back inside it.

The pantsuit-wearing maniac with the bloody fists waltzed around the corner. At the same time, half a dozen more killers emerged from hiding spots behind the purple curtains surrounding them.

They were trapped.

"I told you I found some new friends," the woman shrieked. She gave Holly a neighbourly wave. "Coo-ee! Remember me?"

"Father says not to hurt them too bad," a hulking, bearded behemoth of a man instructed the others. "The heretics can't see the truth if, you know, they can't see."

The circle of grinning psychopaths tightened around them. Fritz brandished his carving knife at the one closest to him, but the man smashed it away with a swing of his broken bowling pin. Holly winced. She could hear the bones in Fritz's hand crack even over the panicked screams of those cowering inside the box.

"Rosie, can you run?" she whispered. "For me?"

"For you, Sis?" Rosie smiled dreamily. "Anything."

"Good girl. Okay. You see that painting of sunflowers over there? On the count of three, we run. One, two—"

Something blunt smacked into the back of her head.

Everything went black.

CHAPTER
TWENTY-FIVE

S he blinked once; the grey-silver floor swam like ripples in liquid mercury.

She blinked twice; the throbbing ache at the back of her head crested and crashed. Holly winced and sucked her teeth as the cries and whimpers of fellow survivors filled the pungent air around her.

Her arms hurt. They weren't bruised, only sore from being raised for so long. She was being dragged by them. Her shoes bounced and skipped across the floor behind her. The more she blinked, the more the black boots of the men 'escorting' her came into focus.

"Rosie?" she asked. The name came out cracked and raspy.

"I'm here, Sis," said the dreamy voice to her right. "I'm here."

Holly turned her head. It felt almost as stiff as her arms, and the way the motion blurred her vision further made her queasy. Her sister was also being pulled along, though judging by the semi-tranquil expression stuck to her face, it wasn't causing her much distress. She didn't appear hurt, though. No more hurt than before, at least. That was good. Holly started to wonder if Rosie's delirium was entirely down to shock, or whether she was beginning to succumb to whatever madness had already infiltrated the rest of the space station's population.

As laborious an ordeal as it was, Holly managed to rotate her head a full one-hundred-and-eighty degrees to face her left. Fritz marched along beside them, eyes down like everyone else, cradling his fractured hand. He looked utterly defeated. Holly didn't blame him. They *were* defeated. Hell, soon they'd be dead.

The mad woman with the bloody fists skipped ahead of the crowd, singing some show tune Holly vaguely recognised. Peering up through the gap between the men pulling her, Holly realised she was being dragged not just forwards, but up a ramp. It had once been another grand staircase but, for some reason Holly's muddled brain struggled to compute, large aluminium panels had been laid down over the steps. Panels from the station's exterior, by the looks of it.

Something had been brought up here, she realised.

Something big.

"I'm sorry I couldn't save you," she whispered to her sister.

"Don't be silly, Holly." Rosie was lost in a daydream. "Maybe I'm sorry I couldn't save *you*, huh?"

Holly opened her mouth to explain the severity of their situation, to try and wake her up from her blithe stupor, but decided that maybe it would be better if her sister wasn't fully lucid when they met their fate.

Their group finally reached the top of the ramp. The ceiling was first to reveal itself – an uninspired grid of girders and pipes and ventilation shafts only acceptable because nobody in that room would ever normally think to cast their gaze upwards. But then the great glass window came into view, slowly unfolding from top to bottom, flanked by enormous peripheral walls painted an impossibly dark purple to resemble the rich, starswept cosmos outside. Vertical beams had been erected around the hall using the observation deck's wooden benches. The greying corpses of dozens of traitors and heretics were pinned to them. Close to a hundred residents and workers from elsewhere around the station gathered in crowds to either side, smiling expectantly.

Observation's massive window had to be twenty metres high, if not more, but even that was scarcely enough to contain the view. Saturnalia's viewing platform kept its gaze fixed permanently on its planetary namesake, a colossal gas giant almost one hundred times the size of humanity's original homeworld. Banded clouds and white storms crossed its murky yellow surface. It was imperious, adamantine, as old as the very heavens in which it lay. Stars and ice particles twinkled around its bulging girth. Even now, her life and sanity both coming to their ends, Holly couldn't help marvelling at its majesty.

Yet it didn't hold her attention for long.

Standing in the centre of the observation deck was a dark monolith, eighteen feet in height and a third as wide. It was unremarkable, save for its cracked and warped texture, and yet Holly found herself compelled to look at it... *into* it... and in its twisted blackness found only echoes of herself. She tried to look away from it, couldn't, and succeeded only when she scrunched up her eyes and focussed instead on her pain.

And soon after, somebody else's.

Fritz was screaming – a trembling snivel that climbed into a tortured caterwaul. He'd wandered free from the group and approached one of the crucifixes. It didn't take much brainpower for Holly to figure out why, even with her head spinning.

"No, no no *no*," he moaned, clawing mindlessly at his face. "Maria... *mein Lieber*... please, no..."

With her head bowed, the woman in the maid's outfit almost looked as if she were gazing down fondly at Fritz from up on her wooden beam. But her face was grey, her eyes as glassy as those of the stuffed animals back in the residential suites, and her jaw hung open in a zombie's yawn. The necklace Fritz had been searching for in his quarters hung around her neck. Holly looked away as much out of disgust as respect. If she were to guess, Maria had been dead for days. Probably ever since this whole nightmare began.

"Not everybody is picked to see the light," said a rich, old, Irish voice. "Some are blind to it. And some choose to fight what they know in their hearts to be true."

A man in a black priest's robe strolled out from behind the monolith, his arms stretched out wide, his pale, veiny fingers poking out like worms from his ample, flowing sleeves. His thin white hair swayed in wisps above his head as if a static charge had been run through him, and his thick beard was coated with flecks of blood and spittle. Eyes that must have once warmed worried hearts now swivelled around the hall, unfocussed, recognising shapes that only he could see.

Father O'Brien, Holly presumed.

"Come, children. Further, further." He beckoned the captured survivors closer to the monolith, as if any of them had any choice. "You are in the presence of celestial gospel, of cosmic divinity. Feel privileged."

The enormous bearded man loomed over Fritz, drowning the engineer in his shadow, and nudged him towards the rest of the group. Fritz shook his head as if refusing, and his mouth opened and closed as if he were having a private conversation with himself, but he took the not-so-subtle cue and stumbled over to where Holly, Rosie and the others had been forced to kneel. He was a man on autopilot. He dropped to the floor alongside her, about half a dozen metres away from the monolith, tears cleaning lines down his dusty, dirt-smeared face, looking almost as lifeless as his wife.

"Fritz?" Holly whispered. "Oh God, Fritz, I'm so sorry."

Her words didn't seem to reach him. Whatever strength and sanity he'd received from his belief in Maria's continued survival was long gone.

"Father O'Brien, please." Holly recognised the man who spoke up from back inside the theatre. "You know us. We're your friends, for goodness' sake! Please let us go. Whatever this is, we won't get in your way, I swear. Right, everyone?"

Everybody not too terrified to speak hurriedly nodded and muttered in the affirmative.

"Oh, would if I could, Mr. Sanghera," Father O'Brien replied with a pleasant smile. "Would if I could. Live and let live, isn't that what I used to teach you? But to deprive you of such a gift... well, a life without light is really no life at all."

A woman ahead of Holly suddenly rocked forwards, clenching her jaw and clutching her head in both hands.

"Christ, that hurts," she screamed. "What the fuck *is* that thing?"

Suddenly, Holly could feel it too – the cold point of an icepick slowly chipping its way into the core of her brain like a psychic lobotomy. The corners of her vision were growing dark – soon, she suspected only the monolith would remain.

Father O'Brien rested a hand against the alien rock. Holly thought she saw a flash of oily blackness splash across the priest's eyes before he spoke, but perhaps that was just her imagination.

Perhaps.

"Beautiful, isn't it? Pure. Primordial. It came to us. It chose us. Of all Earth's children, it chose *us*. And you would spurn its light, why?"

Holly knew she should be planning some kind of escape. Or at least a way to get out of this mess alive, or with her mind intact. Hell, she'd settle for just getting her little sister free of this hellhole. But she was beat. She had nothing left – no energy, not even for her thoughts. Maybe it was easier to give in. More people from Flynn Industries would come to check on Saturnalia sooner or later. If anyone was still alive by the time they did, well, maybe they could be cured of whatever madness plagued them.

"We discovered it suspended in orbit outside the observation window," Father O'Brien continued, caressing it. "Beckoning us. *Singing* to us. We had a scientific responsibility, of course. Did it stem from somewhere deep inside the metallic hydrogen that envelops Saturn's core, far past the helium seas, or from our neighbour, the moon of Titan? We wondered what such a discovery might teach us about our universe... ha! To compare those mortal dreams against what it has already shown us..."

He rested his head against the stone.

"Mr. Yang sent the EVA pod out to retrieve the artefact. The pilot who returned was... different. Enlightened. Yang restrained him, of course, for he was yet to see the same truth. But word spread quickly amongst Saturnalia's people. Something priceless had been discovered, something older than humanity itself. They owned the station, they argued, and by all rights therefore owned whatever was brought aboard. And so, with great reluctance and caution, Yang displayed it for all to see."

The station's former administrator wasn't present in Observation, Holly noticed. She guessed he hadn't let the right kind of light into his heart.

"And see it we did," O'Brien continued. His disciples grinned and chuckled in agreement. "And what else we saw! It gave us sight beyond these mere mortal forms of flesh and their drab, fallible planes. It laid bare the destiny of our kind should we only follow the righteous path. But there were others who feared the transformation, the *evolution* they saw in us. They did not understand the artefact, and so, as with all they do not understand, they sought to destroy it. We stopped them. We stopped *all* of them. And so it showed us what we faithful already knew in our hearts to be true. You either walk in the light... or you are a threat to it."

Father O'Brien grew serious.

"The truth is glorious. It is incontrovertible, undeniable. And now you, if the Menhir chooses, will open your eyes to it too."

The woman with the brain-splitting migraine had stopped rocking back and forth. Still on her knees, she looked over her shoulder at the rest of the crowd. Holly shuddered. Her eyes were barely lucid, but her face had contorted into a deranged grin.

"You should try it," she sighed. "I've never been happier."

"The first of many new converts, I hope," Father O'Brien said proudly. He stepped forward and pulled her away from the crowd. "How wonderful. Sister, come stand over here."

She jostled amongst the attending zealots and the woman with the bloody fists casually wrapped an arm around her shoulders as if they were buddies. Just like that, she was one of them.

"Why did you kill her, Father?" Fritz suddenly asked, the question tumbling out from between his numb, trembling lips. "Why did you kill my Maria? She wasn't a threat to anybody."

Father O'Brien looked down on him with pity.

"Perhaps the Menhir will show you," he replied, waving him forward. "Come, son. I can see the darkness tormenting you. Let its light in."

Holly felt another sharp stab of pain in the centre of her temporal lobe. It was much stronger this time; the icepick had chipped its way to the core. But this time it was accompanied by a flash of mental images, each with a greater clarity and vibrancy than even the photograph tucked inside her back pocket. She saw herself and Rosie as children, as teenagers, as they were right now – at every stage of their lives, wandering down Saturnalia's Main Street, arm-in-arm as sisters. And there, waving to them from the steps behind the intact gates of the residential suites, were their parents – alive, happy, and just how she remembered them looking when they forced her and Rosie on board the Ark ship. No tears this time, though. Even inside these snapshots, she could feel herself smiling from ear to ear, because everything in the universe was exactly how it was supposed to be.

The pain subsided and Holly returned to the Observation deck, sweating and out of breath. This wasn't religion, she realised. Nor had Saturnalia been swallowed by the hungry gulf of its class divide. This menhir *thing* was simply manipulating people, and people were *happy* to be manipulated, because it meant they could believe in whatever they wished to be true. They alone were right, everyone else was wrong. Call it madness, naivety, blind faith – it was human nature, through and through.

"Don't give in to it, Fritz," she yelled. "It only shows people what they want to see."

One of the zealots guarding the captives went to bludgeon Holly into silence, but Father O'Brien raised his hand and she paused with her pipe above her head.

"Our friend here will understand soon enough," he said kindly.

Fritz stood beside Father O'Brien directly before the stone, his body drooping like a marionette. Holly could only see his back. God knew what lies the monolith was showing him. Images of him and Maria together again, most likely. Spinning fantasy into a new reality. Right now, the poor engineer was especially vulnerable. It wouldn't be a difficult conversion.

"Open your mind to it," said the priest. "The Menhir's truth brings us all together as one."

Outside, an uncaring Saturn slowly turned, framing the monolith with a dusty glow. Fritz's left hand dangled by his hip. It kept twitching.

"But you killed my Maria," he said quietly, his voice shaking. "And you know what, Father? Most of the time, the truth – the *real* truth – it hurts."

Fritz reached behind his back and grabbed the wrench tucked into the waistband of his overalls. He swung it around like he was playing for the New York Mets and struck Father O'Brien right across the temple. The priest crashed backwards into the monolith in a flailing tornado of black robes and spraying claret.

Fritz spun around and looked Holly dead in the eye.

"Run!"

CHAPTER
TWENTY-SIX

I f madness hadn't already seized the Observation deck, it did now. The other survivors forced to crouch in front of the blood-splashed artefact must have thought Fritz's command to run was intended for them, because almost every captive immediately screamed and bolted in every direction. Rosie was one of the few who didn't, looking around at the commotion in surprise as if all the noise had woken her from a peaceful slumber.

Holly grabbed her sister under the arms and yanked her to her feet. Together they stumbled towards the exit to Operations – thankfully, Rosie seemed to have regained a modicum of her usual motor functions, even if she wasn't completely lucid – weaving through the panicking survivors and dodging furious attacks from the insane and indoctrinated. They didn't look back. Those still in their right minds were outnumbered and unarmed – this wasn't a fight they could hope to win, with or without Holly's help.

They reached the staircase, the centre of which was still laid out as a ramp using the station's hull panels. Holly decided not to take the steps to either side. They'd build up speed if they ran down the slope, and if they fell – well, it just meant they'd reach the bottom all the faster.

"This way, Rosie," she said. "I'm getting you out of here."

They sprinted down towards the giant circular door at the bottom. The trail of blood and dirt leading back out into the intersection of Operations didn't faze her anymore. There was so much blood everywhere. Her hair had been matted together by quite a bit of her own.

The two halves of the door slid aside and they were met with a gust of cool, aseptic air. Holly shivered. The doors to the various other sections of Operations beckoned, as did the grand staircase that led back down into the Resort District.

"Where are we going?" Rosie asked politely.

It was a good question. Holly had simply wanted to escape – she hadn't put all that much thought into the plan part of it. She couldn't pilot the EVA maintenance vehicle, so that was out of the question. They wouldn't survive for very long in there, anyway. But she did know her way around the station's access tunnels pretty well by now. Could she make it back down to Engineering? Fritz's hiding spot probably hadn't been discovered yet, and there'd been plenty of food and water in there when they left it...

A hand fell on her shoulder. Holly shrieked and spun around, intending to club her assailant with a hammer she no longer had in her possession. But it was only Fritz. He was drenched in sweat, severely out of breath, and sporting a nasty cut above his left eye.

"Escape pods," he wheezed. "Now!"

Holly dragged Rosie into Administration. Her sister stared at the blinking computers in childlike wonderment.

"I don't think I've ever been in here before..."

Holly rushed over to the door through which she first discovered the escape pods. Fritz darted past her.

"Not those ones," he shouted. He punched the button for the next door over. "In here. Pod B5."

The three of them bolted inside the corridor. Rosie gawped at the rows of escape pods. Fritz flicked open a control panel beside the door and started fiddling with its locking mechanism.

"Who had mind-corrupting alien artefact on their bingo card? Fuck me." Holly collapsed against the closest wall and closed her eyes. "So much for *human made, humans saved.* I think I liked it better when we thought the rich and the poor were killing each other."

"Yes, well." Fritz licked his lips as he concentrated on the wiring. "At least this way everyone is as bad as each other."

The door slammed shut again. When Fritz pushed the button to open it, nothing happened. He turned back to the women and nodded.

'Which pod is B5?" Holly asked.

"Erm... that one."

"I thought you said all the escape pods had been vandalised."

"Yeah, I may have stretched the truth just a little bit," Fritz replied, flashing her an exhausted smile. "Yang's terminal showed that this pod was still operational. Mostly. I just didn't want you to leave the station before we found your sister and..."

His words trailed off and his smile faltered. Holly didn't know what to say. Then he tapped the touch-screen of B5's control terminal using the fingers of his own good hand and unlocked the escape pod's door.

"Well, the three of us can still make it, can't we?"

Holly encouraged Rosie into the pod, then climbed in

after her. It was cramped, but no more so than the cabin of the shuttle that brought her to Saturnalia in the first place, and considerably more comfortable. The curved rear of the pod was formed mostly of a padded, cushioned sofa; five sets of straps could be pulled down over the occupants' shoulders. Latched panels lined the rest of the white, plastic walls. They were labelled simply: Food, Sanitation, First Aid. As with the shuttle, a tiny cubicle housed a single chemical toilet with a lid that had to be locked when not in use. Compared to most of Saturnalia's upper sectors, it was a dump – but in truth, it was about as glamorous as one could expect from any vessel smaller than a private ship.

Screams could be heard coursing through the halls of Operations. Fritz hurriedly swung himself through the hatch and started inputting the launch sequence on the internal monitor.

"Can you work it?" Holly asked.

"Should be able to," Fritz replied. "Escape pods are only deployed in emergencies, right? They're not much use if only a trained expert knows how to operate one."

He tapped the screen and glanced at the escape pod's door, expecting it to close. It didn't. The screen flashed red. He tried again, eliciting the same results.

The terrified shrieks and metallic banging grew louder. It sounded like the zealots were inside Administration.

"What's happening, Fritz?" Holly crowded him at the control panel. "Why aren't we leaving?"

"I don't know."

"You said this one was operational!"

"I said it was *mostly* operational! Mostly! I think they only sabotaged the internal launch mechanism."

"Only the launch mechanism?" Holly screamed at him.

"Oh, good! Because launching is just the one thing we need to do, right? That's fucking perfect, Fritz!"

He craned his neck to look at the external control terminal back in the corridor, glanced back at the red warning sign on the screen inside the escape pod.

"Wait there," he said, clambering back out of the hatch. "I might be able to trigger the launch from out here."

"Are you sure this is the right pod?" she called out after him. Rosie also approached the door for a better look.

"Just stay put!"

Fritz tapped away at the external terminal, shaking his head and biting the corner of his lip. He jerked his head to the side as a thunderous banging rattled the corridor's door, then got back to work.

"What is it?" Holly shouted. "What's happening?"

"They're about to break through the door," Fritz replied. "It's fine. I think I've got it."

With a decisive prod of his finger, he input the final launch command. The escape pod's hatch swung shut so quickly it almost took Holly's fingers off. She stumbled backwards into Rosie, then rushed back to the hatch's small, round window.

"Shit. Come on, Fritz. Get this thing open again."

She tried the monitor Fritz had been fiddling with. It really was designed to be idiot-proof, with simple, colour-coded blocks for each task. But when she tapped the button marked OPEN DOOR, it flashed that same red error message. It was as if the escape pod thought they were already out in the vacuum of space.

Fritz squatted down by the porthole.

"What are you doing?" Holly yelled at him. "Stop standing there and *do* something!"

"It's okay," Fritz replied. He smiled sadly. "I've already

triggered the launch sequence. Don't try and cancel it. This is the only way either of us is getting off Saturnalia."

The monitor inside the escape pod beeped. "T-minus thirty seconds to launch," said a calm woman's voice.

"Shut it off and get back inside," Holly insisted. "Maybe it'll work from this end next time."

"No, it won't. We're lucky that pod is still in any state to launch at all."

More banging on the door outside. Holly could hear it even through the hatch, which muffled Fritz's voice and made it sound – and, thanks to the porthole, look – like he was wearing a goldfish bowl on his head.

"Don't say 'we're' lucky – you're on the wrong side of the door! They're going to kill you!"

"Yes, probably." He shrugged. "But that's all right. Really, it is. At least I proved I'm not a coward, right?"

"Fritz..."

"It's okay. I'll be with Maria again soon. I know it, here." He tapped his heart. "We came to this place together. We'll leave here together, too."

The door to Administration crashed open. Holly watched through the tiny porthole as only the slightest glint of surprise crossed Fritz's eyes before the gatecrashers swarmed him. Holly screamed and pounded her fists against the escape pod's hatch. A few of the zealots stopped attacking Fritz and started hammering the walls of their orb instead.

The escape pod suddenly shifted backwards as it aligned itself with the launch tunnel. One of the men trying to break through the hatch tumbled through the emerging gap into the blast-cavity beneath.

"T-minus ten..." said the monitor. "Nine..."

"Shit." Holly threw herself into one of the seats along the

curved sofa. "Rosie." She snapped her fingers at her. "*Rosie!* Get it together. Strap yourself in."

The two sisters secured themselves into spaces beside one another. Unlike those in the shuttle, these seatbelts were more comfortable and didn't require an instruction manual to fit together. Then again, Holly guessed the escape pod wasn't designed to travel as fast or as far as the shuttle, either.

"Two... one..."

The last thing Holly saw before being jettisoned from Saturnalia was Fritz's limp, bloody body being dragged out of view. She scrunched her eyes up tight and grabbed Rosie's hand. Rosie squeezed it back.

The escape pod launched.

Holly and Rosie were forced down into their cushioned seats as their lifeboat rocketed upwards. She couldn't breathe; someone had dropped a breeze block on her ribcage. The plastic panels shook on their latches; the tiny cabin roared with fury. Holly was sure the pod would crash into the end of the tunnel, or be rigged to blow up, or that the window would sprout a crack and they'd be engulfed by the flames of their own launch jets. But then, all of a sudden, the shaking stopped. The roaring quietened. The weight was lifted from her chest, and she felt strands of Rosie's hair tickle her face like long grass swaying in the wind.

She opened her eyes. The view was astounding. A gentle spin had been applied to the pod upon launch, and Holly watched as the scene outside the porthole slowly changed from a dark fabric through which pinpricks of light shone to the glorious swell of Saturn – and the cold, silver and silent space station that orbited it.

It was over. Holly heard laughter and realised it was her own. She'd found her sister and escaped. Saturnalia was nothing but one more glint amongst the great rings circling the gas giant.

Beside her, Rosie cleared her throat and wrinkled her nose. Her eyes brimmed with tears. She wrung and twisted the straps of her seat in growing alarm.

"Er... Holly? Sis?" Her eyes flittered around the cramped cabin. "What the hell are we supposed to do now?"

TWENTY-SEVEN

They spent the best part of six days aboard their fancy lifeboat. Or so they found out later. For all the luxuries with which their escape pod was equipped, nobody had thought to fit it with a damn clock.

Rosie's mental state bettered, then worsened, then balanced out as the days went on. Flashes of memory returned to her, few of them good, none in any chronological order. Her husband was dead, her home destroyed, the life she spent the past decade building torn down. That she was sharing her tragic confinement with her estranged sister was often little solace. Sometimes she would randomly hug Holly and cry with joy; other times, she refused to speak to her, confused as to why Holly had thought it necessary to intrude on her life at all.

"I didn't need rescuing from a life I chose," Rosie had said during one of her particularly bad spells. "This was supposed to be my way out."

"Way out from what?" Holly had replied incredulously.

"Oh, Sis. You and I remember life aboard the Ark quite differently."

Holly's own head cleared the further they got from Saturnalia. It wasn't just the nasty smack to the back of her skull that was bothering her – there had been a dull, gnawing ache deep in her brain ever since she arrived on the space station, scratching at her lobes, tugging at her synapses. It was something she only noticed after it was gone.

The lockers were full of water, vitamins and food sachets that, whilst a far cry from anything found on the menus of the Convivium, were noticeably more flavoursome than that which she'd been served on the old security team's shuttle. There was even a pack of playing cards, though they soon discovered that playing a hand in zero gravity was a lot more trouble than it was worth. They slept strapped into their chairs. Going to the bathroom was a far from dignified experience. By the third day, Holly wished the escape pod had come with a shower installed, too.

The emergency beacon, activated by the escape pod's launch, called out across the stars. All the two of them could do was wait. And hope. Hope their call was heard, hope that someone came to rescue them.

Came to take them home.

Holly marched into the lobby of the Flynn Industries headquarters, took the elevator up to the sixth floor. Her old pass still worked. Nobody had revoked her access yet. But she wouldn't be hanging around for long.

The pen of identical cubicles was just how she left it. Devoid of colour, character, noise save for the steady, mind-numbing tapping of plastic screens. A stale, musky odour squatted in the poorly circulated air. The light was waxy, slightly too bright, and totally artificial – though after her short stint on the largely windowless Saturnalia, uncomfortably familiar.

More than a few beady-eyed colleagues poked their heads above the walls of their plastic cages as she strolled across the front of the office. The tragedies that transpired on board the Saturnalia space station were being kept as secret as the Flynn Industries board could manage, but there'd been no hiding the fact that a UEC rescue team had retrieved Holly from her escape shuttle after spending the best part of a week drifting through the Sol system. Her prolonged absence from her desk never would have gone unnoticed. Her colleagues probably had a million questions. She looked forward to never answering them.

The door to Aria Nicholson's office was closed. She knocked twice, then cracked it open without waiting for an answer.

Her supervisor glanced up from her data pad in surprise. Her expression darkened for just a fraction of a second, but Holly caught it. Then she broke into a fake smile and waved Holly in.

"Bloom, good to see you," she said. "I didn't think you'd be coming back."

It had been a week since the rocket carrying the UEC rescue team had touched back down on New Terra. The return trip had been marginally less arduous than the one that first took her to Saturnalia, but after floating inside the cushioned escape pod for so long, she forgot how bruising actual space travel could be. Rosie had certainly made her feelings on the matter clear after her third round of travel sickness.

"Me neither," Holly replied, tossing a data drive onto

Nicholson's desk. "I thought I'd drop off the Saturnalia report before I left. I'm nothing if not professional."

Nicholson picked up the data drive to study it.

"Saturnalia report. Huh. You know the board will just have everything on here wiped, don't you?"

"Not if my sister has anything to say about it."

"Oh, yes. Your sister, Rosie Flynn. You kept that one to yourself, didn't you?"

"Well, I didn't want all of my success to be put down to nepotism, did I?"

Nicholson opened a drawer in her desk, slipped the drive inside, and then leaned forwards with her fingers steepled.

"So. Tell me, off the record. What really happened in there?"

Holly shrugged.

"Read the report before you submit it if you really want to find out. Everything I know is in there. The easy answer is that some kind of alien artefact corrupted the minds of Saturnalia's residents and bent them to its will. Or the will of whoever originally chiselled it, I guess. When people tried to destroy it, it fought back. But I don't think that's the full story. I think the artefact took advantage of something innate within us. Within *all* of us. Forget politics, forget religion, forget wealth. What really divides us is our curse to always think that we're right and everyone else is wrong, just because we so desperately want whatever we *believe* to also be *true*. Reality casts a dim light against the flames of faith and fantasy. All the artefact did was reflect back to us what we wanted to see. Human nature did the rest." Holly shrugged again. "But hey, I'm just an analyst. What do I know?"

"Hmm. Yeah." Nicholson raised a finely-plucked eyebrow. "I think the UEC will chalk it down to a mind-controlling space rock. Either way, it's a total disaster. Half the residents are dead along with two-thirds of the staff, and almost everybody who's left is undergoing psychiatric treatment. The poor kids they found hiding in the floorspace of the bakery will never be the same. Even without considering the structural damage, I highly doubt Saturnalia will ever open again."

"Look on the bright side," Holly said as she headed for the door. "Everything was already bought and paid for."

"One moment, Bloom."

Holly paused with her hand on the door handle.

"I could fire you, you know. For intercepting private correspondence, *or* for travelling to a restricted space station under false pretences."

"Wouldn't really matter if you did. I've already quit. Well, this job, at least."

"Bad time to be unemployed on New Terra, Bloom. You got something lined up already?"

"Of course. I'm Rosie Flynn's new analytical advisor. She has a majority stake in the company now, after all. Somebody in her position needs all the support she can get."

Aria Nicholson shook her head and broke into a wry smile.

"I wasn't wrong about you, was I? You *do* have the spark. I guess you weren't lying when you told me you wanted to elevate your position within the company."

"That wasn't why I went to get my sister."

"You keep telling yourself that, Bloom. Good luck."

"Yeah, you too, Nicholson."

She shut the door behind her and headed straight for the elevator doors, purposefully avoiding making eye contact with the half a dozen pairs that slowly cropped up from inside the grid of cubicles. She rode the elevator down to the ground floor and passed through the automated security gates.

Something kept her from leaving. She crossed to the nearest trash receptacle, took off the security pass from around her neck and binned it, and then marched triumphantly through the office building's main doors.

It was a sunny day, and a quick glance at her data pad told her it was 9:38am. Her stomach rolled. She'd slept in and skipped breakfast. Maybe she should try that bagel place she always used to pass on her way to work. She could probably afford it now.

Mustn't be late for her meeting with Rosie at eleven, though. There was a whole new world in which to invest. A few recommendations already came to mind.

She put on her sunglasses as she descended the steps of the headquarters and smiled.

For the first time since leaving Earth with her sister, Holly's future looked bright.

THANK YOU FOR READING!

You may have finished *Saturnalia*, but there are lots more stories set in the same universe. If you enjoyed this book, I think you'll love *The Final Dawn* – a bestselling Space Opera series about Earth's evacuation and one unlucky man's epic exploration of the cosmos.

Alternatively, you can choose your next adventure from my full catalogue of books at the website below.

www.twmashford.com

BOOKS IN THE "DARK STAR PANORAMA" UNIVERSE

Final Dawn Series

- The Final Dawn
- Thief of Stars
- A Dark Horizon
- The New World
- The Tin Soldiers
- Ghost of the Father
- The Stellar Abyss
- The Edge of Night
- The Fatal Dark

War for New Terra Series

- Sigma
- Iron Nest
- Royal Blood

Standalone Novels

- Saturnalia

WANT AN EXCLUSIVE FINAL DAWN STORY?

Building a relationship with my readers is one of the best things about writing. Every now and then I send out newsletters with details on new releases, special offers and other bits of news relating to my books.

And if you sign up to the mailing list I'll even send you a **FREE** copy of *Before the Dawn*, an exclusive prequel to *The Final Dawn* – a series set in the same universe as Saturnalia.

Not bad, eh?

Sign up today at www.twmashford.com.

ENJOY THIS BOOK? YOU CAN MAKE A BIG DIFFERENCE.

Reviews are the most powerful tool in my arsenal when it comes to getting attention for my books. As an indie author, I don't have quite the same financial muscle as a New York publisher. But what I *do* have is something even more effective:

A committed and loyal bunch of readers.

Honest reviews of my books help bring them to the attention of other readers.

If you've enjoyed this book I would be very grateful if you could spend just five minutes leaving a review (it can be as short as you like) on the book's Amazon page.

Thank you very much.

BOOK CLUB QUESTIONS

Do you think Saturnalia's comms were sabotaged, or were external messages blocked by the artefact? How does this lack of communication reflect the breakdown of dialogue in modern socio-political discourse?

Why do you think Holly really wanted to bring Rosie home? Was it for her sister's sake, or her own? Is Holly as guilty of blurring fantasy and reality as the residents?

The artefact only shows the zealots what they want to see. How does this behaviour reflect the echo chamber effect seen in many physical and online communities?

Are there any aspects of your own life that you'll believe and defend without question? (We all have them!)

ABOUT THE AUTHOR

Tom Ashford lives just outside London, England with his wife Jenny and extremely needy cat, Kathleen.

An avid movie buff and video game addict, Tom loves all things science fiction. That's why he started the *Dark Star Panorama* – a shared universe full of epic spacefaring stories including the *Final Dawn* and *War for New Terra* series.

His favourite authors are Terry Pratchett and Stephen King.

Send him an email at tom@twmashford.com. He'll enjoy the attention.

facebook.com/TWMAshford

instagram.com/ashfordtom

Printed in Great Britain
by Amazon

24876137R00155